TO DESTROY BETELGEUSE

"They wouldn't believe me, and they left me to rot on this damned world. Now they are seeking me out because they are afraid, because the Times are drawing nearer and the Masters are grumbling, because they are discovering the Accursed Worlds one by one."

The old man looked up at Algan.

"Who are you," he asked in his cracked voice, "that you should have in your possession the chessboard of the Masters? During the course of my long life, I've seen it just three times. Once, it was the one you have, or one exactly like it, and the other two times I saw it etched on the black walls of those damnable citadels. Who are you? Are you one of their men? Have you come to take my soul, as you did from all the other poor spacemen you buried alive?"

"I'm just looking for a weapon to destroy Betelgeuse," said Algan simply. **"I'm counting on you."**

STARMASTERS' GAMBIT

Gerard Klein

Translated by C. J. RICHARDS

DAW BOOKS, INC.

DONALD A. WOLLHEIM, PUBLISHER

1301 Avenue of the Americas
New York, N. Y.   10019

Cover art by Kelly Freas.

To JACQUES BERGIER

FIRST PRINTING, AUGUST 1973

1 2 3 4 5 6 7 8 9

PRINTED IN U.S.A.

CHAPTER I

The Recruiters

He was thirty-two years old and his name was Jerg Algan. Most of his life had been spent on the Earth, where he'd roamed over the planet. He had glided across the seas on rickety hydrofoils, flown over whole continents in obsolete planes left over from the last century; he had sunbathed on the beaches of Australia; he had hunted the last lions in Africa before the desert plateau had tumbled into the ocean.

His achievements had been negligible. He had never left the Earth. He had traveled through the stratosphere. Between trips he lived in Dark, supporting himself doing odd jobs as it was possible to do in large cities.

Dark was, in fact, the sole remaining city on the Earth. It had a population of thirty million and was the last resort in all of the Galaxy for men of his sort. So long as they went quietly about their business, the Psychological Police left them alone. By virtue of its situation and antiquity, Dark, despite its small size, had become one of the most important ports of that section of the Galaxy. Here, trafficking in all sorts of commodities was unrestricted. All the known species, and some unknown as well, could be bought; even forbidden imports, presumed to be dangerous, could be procured. All the drugs concocted for humans, as well as for other breeds, were obtainable in Dark. It was rumored that even slaves were available. Dark was the never-ending scandal of the Galaxy.

Algan had had his ups and downs. He couldn't remember ever working more than three months at the same job,

nor having sold the same commodity twice. He had never
had any run-in with the Psychological Police, but that
hadn't been entirely his doing.

He was now looking for something else to do: a chance
to explore a corner of the Earth as yet unknown to him.
There were still a few unexpected opportunities to be
found in the section of the old stellar port which handled
only the traffic for the near planets: perhaps he'd run into
an old crank on his first visit to the Old Planet who wanted to visit ancient ruins; or get his clutches into an obses-
sive hunter consumed with the ambition of adding a Terrestrial rabbit to his trophies; or, best of all, find some lost
member of a scientific expedition who, between a couple
of drinks, would pay to find out what he knew about the
customs of the inhabitants of the Earth.

Algan went into *Orion's Sword,* a tavern whose very
name caused, quite unfairly, a shudder to run through the
high-minded. He sat in the darkest corner and ordered a
drink. He slouched at his ease, never taking his eyes off
the door. Orion's Sword, which gave the place its name,
swung over the entrance. It was a long shiny stem of steel,
sharp as a needle, antenna-like, decorated with curious
sparkling moldings. Had it really served as a weapon, millions of years ago, in another world? No one knew. It
could have been just an artifact.

The bar was still almost deserted and surprisingly silent.
Even the zotl presses seemed muffled.

Algan clinked some silver on the table.

"One zotl," he said.

The sight of the heavy pistons crushing the hard root as
it slowly lost its color, while the juice foamed out, gave
him almost as much pleasure as drinking the amber liquid.
Zotl root was one of the few legal sources of drugs in certain sections of the Galaxy. Its effect varied with the individual. Sometimes it produced sensations of power. Its effect was comparable to cenesthetic frenzy, the nervous
mental state which is the result of the crossing of nerve
ends that makes sounds visible and colors audible.

Algan slowly drained his glass. Every time he drank zotl
he had the same vision: a gray desert under a low green
sky spangled with the iridescent outlines of moving rocks,

which regrouped themselves to the rhythm of the ages. Distant, invisible suns played strident music. It was a peaceful spectacle, outside of time.

When he opened his eyes again the bar was half-full. There were men from every corner of the universe: merchants from Rigel wearing their metal shirts; tremendously tall, thin navigators from Ultar moved clumsily, hampered by Terrestrial gravity; small Xiens with blond hair and speckled eyes; bald men from Aro with pupil-less eyes deep as wells, under bulging foreheads, their complexions livid, almost greenish.

Dress and colors varied: some were bright, some gaudy, some dull. Weapons had a nightmarish quality about them. *Orion's Sword* proffered a small cross section of the sort of carnival that undulated through Dark when a fleet of merchant ships sailed into the stellar port.

Accents ran the gamut from guttural to musical, but everyone there spoke the old space language, a bastard mixture of all the languages of the Earth.

Someone sat down next to Jerg: a sturdy Earthling with a deep tan and a paunch filled with the good food available in this Galaxy.

"Would you like to do some traveling, Mack?" the man asked, looking at Algan.

"It all depends where," replied Algan, guardedly.

"Take your pick; you can go where you like. A zotl?"

"I'll take the zotl anyway," said Algan.

They drank and remained silent for a bit.

"There are many beautiful worlds in space," said the fat Earthling dreamily.

"Are there?"

"Young man, when I was your age I had already been to about fifty planets. But maybe you have too . . . ? You're between expeditions, aren't you? Space isn't an adventure anymore, is it? Another zotl?"

"I've never left the Earth," Algan said slowly, "and I don't want to. There's nothing like this green Earth; you can have all those worlds whirling about in space. . . . Thank you for the zotl. But it takes more than a zotl to put out the sun, as the saying goes. Isn't that right?"

"Sure."

They were silent for a moment. Algan scanned the
small weasel eyes deep-set in fleshy slits. There was a
gleam in them that he did not like.

"I suppose you're a trader."

The Earthling gave a coarse laugh.

"You can call it that, young man. I'm a sort of trader.
Business is a bit tight on Earth at this moment, isn't it?"

Politeness was absolutely essential in space and in ports.
Jerg Algan understood the value of caution, so he had cultivated exquisite manners, and the better part of good
manners consisted in the art of never baldly asking questions.

"Yes, rather. Goods are getting scarce."

The fat businessman again laughed coarsely. Jerg chose
to join in. That made the fat Earthling laugh even more.
His eyes kept disappearing behind fleshy folds of fat. Algan suddenly stopped laughing.

"Are you looking for something on Earth? I know it
like my pocket. Perhaps I can help."

"Perhaps you can. A zotl, my boy?"

Algan disliked the familiarity of the fat man's tone, but
the zotl excused it. Looking inwardly at his dream, soaring
over a gray desert, he could hear his companion's clucking
noises crashing down like a sudden darkness, smothering
the song of aerial suns.

"Sure, you can help me, my boy. Just sign this and
you'll see new places."

"Where are you going?" asked Algan thickly.

"Where duty calls," came from the depths of a fold of
fat. He felt something damp on his fingertips, then was
aware that they were being crushed on a hard surface.

"Is he ever plastered!" said a strange voice. He opened
his eyes. Someone placed between his fingers a cylinder
made of something soft. He didn't know what it was. He
was flying between pearly cliffs under a low green sky.

"Write your name, chum," said an affectionate voice
which he could see being written in the clouds in a flowery
script. "You want to travel, you're dying to travel. Write
your name."

Large luminous stones were writhing to the rhythm of

unstable millennia, like tentacles trying to put out the light of the whole universe.

"Sign, chum; one more try."

He tried to pull himself together, to make his fingers hold the little cylinder. He began to write, but it was difficult because his half-shut eyes could perceive the colors only as sounds.

"One more try."

He stuck out his tongue and began to drool. Someone took hold of his arm and said:

"OK."

Algan dropped his hand; it was so heavy he thought his arm was going to come off. He felt himself falling between endless pearly cliffs, dragged down by the leaden weight of his right hand. Then he fell forward. His fingers drummed on the hard surface of the table. His eyes, riveted on the iridescent glass, perceived an increasingly intense and strident sound. He was plunging into a pearly well, down, down into green water under a green sky; it was like a pearly cylinder with a green floor and a green ceiling which were coming closer and closer. The pearly wall was now only a narrow strip between those green areas, nothing more than a thread. Then the well exploded.

He sat up suddenly, lights still flickering in his eyes. He instinctively touched his armpit with his right hand; then he snorted like someone coming out of the water.

There was no one next to him. The fat Earthling with the sausage-like fingers could well have been a dream.

He raised his hand and snapped his fingers.

"A drink."

He emptied the glass in one gulp and felt better. He got up and tried to walk. His legs felt as though he'd been lying down for centuries. He had drunk too much zotl. He felt around in his pockets and left a handful of coins on the table, then he went toward the door. Someone greeted him as he went by and he responded with a weary gesture. He was stumbling and as he was about to fall steadied himself by clutching the doorknob.

The thick damp air of Dark engulfed him as he went out. He blinked several times.

Painfully, he walked along the badly lit street. His feet slithered along pavements worn down by thousands of boots, but his well-trained eyes unconsciously searched the dark corners. Dark was a safe city but only up to a point, and it was better never to find out what that exact point was.

He had no place to go. He thought of spending the night in some section of the old town, a place where one could lean one's back against a corner and doze, hand on pistol butt.

The lights of the Old Stellar Port guided him. He wove in and out of doorways, followed dark passages between houses that were older than the port itself, avoided openings that were too well-lit. He occasionally stumbled and made use of the brief lights from outgoing ships to pick his way along.

A sudden noise made him prick up his ears.

"Now," a voice shouted.

Several men jumped him. He had not seen them approaching and tried to fight his way out of the fog clouding his mind. Just as they were about to grab him he slipped to the ground, then ran between their legs. It worked. He started to run, trying to see who had attacked him.

His boots echoed on the pavement. He couldn't hope to shake off his pursuers. An open doorway in this section of town would be almost as dangerous as the street. His only real chance was to come upon a patrol of the Psychological Police. But the police seldom ventured out at night in the Old Stellar Port, not because they were concerned with their own safety but because there was actually no need for them. The inhabitants of the old town did not ask for the protection of the Psychological Police and the Psycho left them pretty well alone. This was the result of an ancient tacit understanding which gave the people of the ten puritan planets a chance to criticize the vices of the Old Planet.

Algan's right hand went up to his armpit and he caressed the sheath of his radiant. Murder was a serious matter, not to be committed except under extreme provocation. Explanations to the Psycho about legitimate self-defense would fall on deaf ears.

He looked over his shoulder and saw that his attackers were very close. They ran almost noiselessly. He could see four shadows. Perhaps others followed. In any event, the struggle was over even before it had begun unless he used his weapon.

Swerving suddenly, he turned into an adjoining alley which led to the Stellar Port by an enormously wide staircase. But he knew he would never reach the bronze doors. He heard his pursuers laugh. Goaded, he went faster. For one second he thought he'd shaken them on the winding stone staircase, but there was no place to go. He could only leap from step to step, fleeing between those blind walls, under a thin ribbon of sky and stars, trying to figure out who they were, why they wanted him, and where they were now.

He was rapidly getting winded. His right hand touched the radiant in its sheath. Perhaps he ought to stop and fight. Or was he nearer the port than he thought? They didn't give him time to choose. They shot first. They didn't want to kill him, but a large sticky ball hit him in the nape of the neck while steely strips furled themselves around his legs. He fell forward, his hands groping for the ground. He tried to roll up in a ball, bouncing from step to step along the walls and at the same time reaching for his radiant. But the blow on his neck was paralyzing him and more strips fettered his arms. He managed to pull out his radiant and squeezed the trigger. Nothing happened. He squeezed the butt against the palm of his hand, but there was no shot. As he sank into darkness he felt the butt of his weapon. It had no loading clip.

He flung the weapon away and it bounced from step to step. Then hands ran over him.

"That's him."

"OK. Go to it."

A cupping glass was put against his right ear. The thin ribbon of sky and stars began to revolve and turn green while the dark walls became lighter and lighter, taking on a pearly gray hue.

"Good night," he mumbled and fell asleep.

He was drifting on a pearl-gray cloud and wondered what he was doing there. He woke up, and at once felt for his pistol; it was gone. Then he realized that he was lying naked on a cot in a windowless, white-walled room.

He pushed himself up on an elbow. He had to sort this out. Algan dimly remembered having been in a fight the night before. Perhaps the Psychological Police had picked him up. He did not like the idea. Unless he had been wounded and been brought to the port hospital for treatment. Yet he was feeling in splendid form.

As he thought the situation over, he realized that the room looked exactly like the ones in the Stellar Port which he had occasionally visited. There was nothing intrinsically worrisome about it except that it seemed to have no aperture: no door, no window, no trapdoor. He was not unduly concerned; since he had got in, he would certainly find a way out. On the other hand, the theft of his clothes was decidedly irritating. But was it really a theft?

He tried to recall the last thing that had happened to him. As he unconsciously rubbed his head behind his right ear he suddenly remembered that he had been given the bell treatment. That in itself was more worrisome than the loss of his clothes. As far as he knew only the police used those instruments and they were so well-guarded that an ordinary gang of thieves would not have access to them. He undoubtedly was in the hands of the Psycho.

Algan was reassured with the thought that if they had wanted to kill him they could have done so much more easily when he was unconscious.

He lay back on the cot and waited. He needed more information to plan either defense or escape. And if the Psycho was out to get him, they had at least five charges against him; he did not even have to open his mouth.

The wall facing him lighted up and became transparent. He could see the Stellar Port now. In the back, among the high prows pointing skyward, at the very end of the huge cement plain, gleamed the great bronze doors which separated order and space from the chaos of the city.

The wall on his right opened up like a piece of cloth being torn.

"Get up and go down the hall," a voice said.

He did so. The feebly lit corridor closed behind him. It was a one-way passage.

He reached a small, totally dark room. As he was trying to get his bearings he felt something warm winding around his arm. He put up no resistance. He felt the slight sting from the hypodermic needle. Then a gentle rain fell on him. Heat from invisible rays dried him off. The wall in front of him opened again and he went down a wide brilliantly lit corridor which led to a small room. There were clothes hanging on the wall. Algan noted that they were a navigator's outfit.

"Get dressed," said a voice.

He quickly donned the clothes, uttering not one word of useless protest, and set forth down another corridor. The building seemed to be made of some kind of malleable material which lent itself to partitioning into vacuums. Then, suddenly, the walls of the long winding corridor sprang open and Algan stopped, blinking; he seemed to be suspended over space, afloat, in broad daylight, three rocket-lengths above the port. Or so he thought. Actually he was in a large room one whole wall of which was an enormous window that opened on the working part of the port. As his eyes became accustomed to the light he looked around him. A man in a blue shirt was seated behind a huge white desk. He seemed to be waiting.

"Good morning," he said. "Go ahead and admire the port. It's as good a beginning as any."

Algan did not immediately answer. He was, actually, fascinated by the port and the huge ships but he also did not know what to say. This was his first visit to the Stellar Port. People like him were ordinarily kept out.

"I'm ready to talk now," he said quietly.

"I'm glad you're taking it like that," the man in blue replied. "Usually I have to do so much arguing with people who come here for the first time that my job becomes almost unpleasant. Please sit down."

Algan settled into a large white chair.

"I'm listening."

The man in blue looked somewhat embarrassed.

"I thought you'd have some questions."

"Well, I'm hungry," said Algan.

He was in no hurry for explanations. He was enjoying the chair, the rug with its complicated pattern, the magnificent white desk, and especially the view of the Stellar Port.

"Just as you like," said the man in blue and he pushed a button.

He watched Algan eat, without a word. When Algan had finished, he got up and faced the bay.

"What's your name?" asked Algan, "and why am I here?"

"One thing at a time," replied the man in blue. His searching gray eyes scanned Algan's face. "My name is Tial, Jor Tial. I don't suppose that means much to you. You seem resigned to your fate."

"What fate?" asked Algan coldly. He hoped his nervousness would not show through.

"A marvelous fate," said Tial, with a sweeping gesture that encompassed the room, the port, and the rockets.

"The conquest of space."

"You're joking," said Algan. "I'll never leave the Earth."

"Come, come," said Tial, "don't talk like that. Did you or did you not sign up?"

"Sign up?" echoed Algan.

He suddenly understood. He had been had by a recruiter. The fat Earthling of the night before had gotten him drunk to extort his signature and now he was committed to space, to any planet whatever, after an interminable cruise on a broken-down ship. Anger flooded him. He had heard stories of this, in the Old Port, but he had never paid any attention to them. When anyone disappeared from an old section of Dark, no questions were asked; the missing person was just as likely to turn up a year later, rich enough to buy half a continent on the Old Planet, as he was to simply vanish into the thick air of Dark.

"I see that you follow me. Perhaps some of the details escape you? I can read you the contract. Usually the signatories accept it, hm ... let's say, trustingly. They don't even bother to read the provisions. But I can assure you they are worth it."

"It's against the law," said Algan. "I'm not going to knuckle under. There's still some justice on the Earth."

"Of course," said Tial. "And there are judges who can determine whether or not a contract has been properly executed."

"It was extortion," said Algan. "I assume I'm not telling you anything you don't know.

"The judges would be very happy to hear about this. Extortion, you say. By the use of force? Are you quite sure?"

"There's no question of force; I was drugged."

"Against your will?"

"Not exactly. And anyway, you know better than I what happened. All I want is a fair trial; I'll bring charges."

"I should be delighted to give you some advice before you do anything," said Tial.

He spoke coolly and evenly. Algan thought to himself that his case must be weak.

"I presume you admit you drugged yourself. You claim someone took advantage of your condition to make you sign this paper. Is that correct?"

"Not quite," said Algan. "A man offered me several zotls. He seemed anxious to have me drink with him. I didn't want to be unfriendly. Then the stinker took unfair advantage. I suppose he gets something out of this small-time deal."

"You willingly accepted this . . . drug, didn't you?"

Algan agreed.

"You admit having taken more than enough to lose control."

"I don't see what you're getting at."

"Just this: drugs are illegal. Losing control is illegal. I'm willing to believe in the existence of this man. Can you bring him to me? I imagine that the Psychological Police might try to find him for you, but you know that its policy is not to interfere with the people in the Old Port. People like you. Within certain limits, of course. So, do you prefer to be arrested by the Psychological Police for drug abuse and be judged by a jury freshly recruited from the Puritan Planets or will you accept the terms of the con-

tract? I imagine the jury would sentence you to a few
years of hard labor on a new planet. There isn't much
sympathy, you know, for drug addiction among the inhabitants of the Puritan Planets. Wouldn't you rather spend
ten glorious years in space, at government expense, being
handsomely paid? You like adventure, I think. Don't look
back, look forward."

"Very clever," said Algan. "I suppose everyone is in on
this: the Psychological Police, the port authorities, the
space program, and even the government itself. I just say
'Good-bye,' and leave."

He got up, his eyes never wavering from the distant
lights that shone on the prow of a ship. Beyond the bronze
gates the city spread out on the hills, a teeming, disorderly
city made up of multicolored cubes piled up haphazardly—the city which he would not see again for ten
years. A now inaccessible city. Dozens of light-years of
space and emptiness already lay between him and Dark—
hundreds of suns, the possibility of shipwrecks, of unexpected dangers, of unknown, hostile and powerful beings.

And behind the city were the green oceans and the
green plains of the Earth, the inscrutable ruins of its civilizations submerged by a tide of moss, invaded by the great
northern glaciers, its cities dead and their secrets forever
lost. There couldn't, Algan said to himself, there couldn't
be in the universe two planets like the Earth. Something
welled up inside him, a need for revenge; it was a seed
that was to grow during the years spent in emptiness; it
would explode one day and destroy this port, this cold in-
humanity of the Galactians. For a long time he had believed that the Galactians were coldly unconcerned with
the inhabitants of Earth. He would see to it that they paid
when their time came. Only it was too early now, much
too early.

"I've been kidnapped," said Algan in a strangled voice.
"I've been kidnapped. I did not come here of my own free
will. You'll admit that."

"OK, if you want to quibble, you've been kidnapped.
Officially you were picked up by a squad of the Psychological Police and it was only because of your contract that
you were brought here. Under ordinary circumstances

you'd have been tried. But the police officials generously agreed you were entitled to celebrate your departure and they were willing to look the other way. Of course, if you lodge a complaint, they will have to speak up. Believe me, they would rather not."

"If the people of the Galaxy knew how pioneers are recruited," said Algan, "if only they knew!"

"Lots of people do know, but the word of an inhabitant of old Dark does not carry much weight in space. I'd bet they'd laugh at you if you told your story. Unless they beat you up when they learn where you come from. The people of the Galaxy take a dim view of backward people like you."

Algan leaned against the large window. He was consumed with fury. He wanted to hurl himself through the glass onto the porcelain ground a thousand feet below. He wanted to see the ships explode and burn and sailors run in every direction, to see the port in ruins while the city, in the shelter of the large bronze gates, looked on peacefully.

Space was a prison and he knew it. He was going to roam for ten years in this prison. Rage and anxiety welled up inside him. He could see in his mind's eye the shining gates of the old free city, hear the rumblings of the ancient and savage life on Earth.

"I know just how you feel," said Tial, "I've seen others, but none quite like you. Most of them scream, shout, threaten, beg. But at the end of three months they feel at home in space. I hope you will, too. Frankly, I'm not sure you will. I hope that somewhere else, on another world, you'll find something similar to this city. I think this one will be very different when you come back in a thousand years."

Algan turned slowly. His eyes shone. One thousand years. It was the fall, the flight into time that he dreaded most; he had never wanted to talk about it. Ten light-years there and one thousand years here. The port would be unchanged, but the city would have disappeared.

"I'll be dead when you come back, that is, if you want to see the Earth. And everyone here will have forgotten me. I hope you will no longer hate me then. In any event, it will not matter in the least. There will be other men, and they will be doing the same simple and difficult things. Sometimes I say to myself that we are lost, not so much in space as in time. Two thousand five hundred years ago, when men first started their voyages of exploration on the Earth, in ships that were wind-propelled, the distance from one place to its antipode was almost as insurmountable to the explorers as the walls of a cell are to a prisoner. Yet now we roam amid the stars. But we are still prisoners of time, more than ever."

"Stop it, stop it."

The sound of those years going by was like the sound of grains of sand tapping against the sides of an hourglass. This was senseless. One thousand years. Glaciers could spread, oceans rise or dry up. The people he knew on Earth would be dead. In the new worlds, everyone lived alone, worked, traded within his own time span. Ships came in and left with the flow and ebb of the years. On the Puritan Planets marriage was forbidden by law because of its immoral consequences; one month of traveling made a son older than his father.

This was understandable. Men were thrown like grains of sand against the stars. They were so weak, so alone.

But he, Algan, was the product of the old Earth. This couldn't be happening to him. He couldn't accept it. His universe was a limited one along a curved horizon; it held lifelong friendships, an old family house, and the land of his forefathers.

"A backward, bestial point of view," sneered the people on the Puritan Planets.

Maybe. Maybe they were right. Maybe man had to change, broaden his views to keep up with his new environment, the Galaxy; much of it was still unexplored after five centuries of space history.

But this was the Future, and like all the inhabitants of ancient cities, like the inhabitants of the Earth who were universally despised, Algan felt himself to be a man of the Past.

"I don't like all the methods of the government," Tial said gently, "but in some ways I think they are good. I, too, am a man of the Past, in my way, which is different from yours, because I wasn't born on this planet. I'm trying to understand you. I know that after me there will be other men who will deal more harshly with the people from the old cities; these men will no longer know anything of the glory of the Earth. I want you to realize this. People like you, Jerg, are condemned for at least one thousand years. One thousand years in this world. When you come back there will be no one who can understand you. But perhaps some of the new planets will have a history by then. A history that is different, slower-moving, more peaceful than the Earth's, but a history nonetheless. As yet, there are so few of us in space. There are more inhabitable worlds in the Galaxy than there are men. Our empire is so fragile. That's why we are forced to send out, so far away, even those who don't want to leave their world. We are spread awfully thin. Try to understand, Jerg."

I have one thousand years to destroy this, Algan thought. *One thousand or ten; it comes to the same thing.*

A long vibration shook the port. A spaceship was rocketing up from a fiery pad. The sky seemed to darken as the ship rose majestically into the atmosphere. When it reached a height of one thousand kilometers, in an almost total vacuum, its reactors would go out and its nuclear propeller would take over. It would speed up almost to the velocity of light—and time for its passengers would come to a stop—and then it would leap into lateral space and there, motionless, during its crew's long sleep, it would drift, outside of time, carried along by one of the great currents of the universe toward its distant and perhaps still unexplored destination.

"A pleasant trip, Algan," said Jor Tial.

"Thank you," Algan replied coldly. But his eyes were not on Tial's; they were searching the sky.

CHAPTER II

The Stellar Port

There were as many invisible threads crisscrossing the universe as there were possible trajectories for a ship. These threads made up something like a canvas and each knot in the canvas was a world, a port. The oldest of these stellar knots, the one from which had sailed the first ships in quest of unimaginable worlds, was the port of Dark. It had been like a spore explosion in those heroic times. Expansion had slowed down in the course of centuries. Not that all the worlds had been explored or that all the explored worlds were inhabited, but because humanity was thinning out. Whole systems were inhabited by only a few families. The most densely populated planets had less than a hundred thousand inhabitants, although there were a few cities in the Galaxy with a population of over fifty million.

It was a time of paradoxes. Not the least of these was the vastness of these cities and the deserted planets. But the traffic of a port, because of its size, required the presence of ever-increasing numbers of men. Machines had been the beginning of a solution. There had been cities of a hundred million inhabitants spread over an entire continent during the heroic times, when for one single man in a spaceship ten thousand men were required on the Earth for the maintenance and repair of the port equipment. But the machines had made it possible to send forth most of the inhabitants of the cities to conquer new worlds. The most ancient cities, like Dark on the Earth, Tugar on Mars, Olnir on Tetla, were only shadows of the gigantic capitals they had once been. Those had been and still were, though widely separated, times of conquest and glory. A man could be his own master, but his life was not worth very much.

Sometimes an entire stellar region sank into silence. It might be a century before the fate of its inhabitants was known. Sometimes they had disappeared altogether and the planet would be classified as dangerous. At other times it was only that they had given up all technological civilization and had simply neglected to turn on their transradios. Sociologists would study these neo-primitives with great interest when their attention was not taken up by the number of worlds and societies which grew up, lived, and died.

Humanity flocked into space, but it also became lost in Time. The planets themselves did not experience the passing of time at the same speed: this varied according to their density or the rate of speed at which they revolved around their axes or their distance from the center of the Galaxy. And those segments of space trips which took place at the speed of light presented odd chronological pitfalls to travelers.

History, as a continuous passing of time, no longer had any meaning. During the five centuries of conquest, as measured in Earth time, history had been a sort of fibrous matter in which it was difficult to discern cause and effect. Wars no longer had any meaning. The central government, whose seat was on a giant planet near Betelgeuse, was an effective and lasting symbol both in space and time, a symbol of unity which local authorities called upon. It seemed as though the rays of the enormous red star which was visible from one end to the other of the human Galaxy carried far and wide the will of central authority. Actually the governing planet did not revolve around the red giant but around a lesser, neighboring star, but the frightened or surprised looks of those who feared or admired the center of the largest human civilization turned instinctively toward Betelgeuse. Its name was whispered as if the brilliance of that star were indeed an indication of the power of its neighbors.

However, had new cultures and civilizations grown up

on each planet, the central government could not have lasted nor kept up its influence.

But that distortion in time, experienced by all human societies which depended upon intersidereal voyages, had prevented the rise of individualism. There was a traditional loyalty throughout the Galaxy to the central government in Betelgeuse because its very endurance represented the only security in these times of permanent dislocation.

The central government sent its officials, its researchers, and its pioneers into all the know worlds of the Galaxy. When they came back, bringing information that was already centuries old, the men in Betelgeuse who were responsible for the destiny of the Galaxy were no longer there. The very names of those who had made the arrangements for their trip were, more often than not, forgotten. But it was immaterial. Data piled up in the giant memory banks of the computers of Betelgeuse; plans that were to be put into effect five hundred years later in some distant section of the Galaxy were drawn up to the last detail.

In order to survive, Man had to know the Galaxy well. The greatest risk he ran was overlooking danger. He had to get used to the idea of danger without ever forgetting its presence. A frighteningly large number of the early explorers had died either because they had not seen the threat to their safety or because they had been too panic-stricken to react defensively. The task of the central government was to set up a training program that would insure the survival of the largest possible number of explorers.

At first Algan thought that he would not survive the training program. Before he had even left the port, while he was working in huge caves, he thought he'd never again see Dark. But the biologists and psychologists had carefully worked out their programs to conform to the limits of human endurance. Space itself has little to do with those limits.

The tests dealt with both the physical and mental endurance of the trainees.

The first time that Algan was tied up in a large arm-

chair he thought it was funny. By the end of the third
minute he was yelling: "Let me out of here. Stop the machine."

But they went right on while he damned them. They
knew how Algan felt because they too had gone through
it. They also knew what was Algan's only hope of es-
caping madness in certain situations, and were aware that
later he would consider these conditions pleasant and rest-
ful compared to what was still to be endured. They hoped
for his sake that they had not made a mistake when they
had examined him.

Algan felt as though he had fallen into an endless dark
space where not a single star shone. He kept falling. His
stomach turned over. His heartbeats, regulated by the
chair's electrodes, sped up.

Algan yelled: "Let me out. Stop."

He kept falling. It was a simple fall, but into the void.
There was nothing to catch hold of, to claw at. He was
conscious, every moment, that he was going to crash on
an immense dark body which he sensed was just under
him. But the end of the fall, delayed second by second,
never came. He thought he'd gone blind.

At about the fourteenth minute he stopped yelling because his throat had become too dry to let out a sound.
He knew he had just crossed the limits of the universe. He
knew now that he would go on falling. There was no longer any point in his being afraid because something worse
than fear had taken its place in his mind.

At about the sixteenth minute he felt as though he had
become a mere point. He tried to remember the time
when he had had hands and legs he could move, but it
was too long ago and too unreal.

At about the eighteenth minute, he thought he was
swelling up.

Being a point of expansion was an intolerable sensation.
He felt as though he were occupying, as he kept falling,
an infinite amount of space, and all the while his nerves
were being stretched in every direction.

At about the twenty-first minute he felt himself exploding.
Countless particles of himself flew about beyond imaginable space. He became an infinitely stretched fog. His mind

tried to follow each of those particles and to hold them,
but he wore himself out in vain; he could not do it. Then
he gave up.

There was no longer anything coherent or ordered
about Algan. He was nothing but chaos and confusion.
Something less than half an hour of total falling had been
too much for him. He felt destroyed, disintegrated. With
what little consciousness remained to him, he understood
that the universe was hostile, and this understanding
restored some strength to him. A core of intelligence, supported by this last recognition, began to reorganize his
scattered memories, his old experiences. A flicker of hatred began to burn in his brain. Suddenly the fall seemed
unimportant to him. He slowly found the path back to his
own nerves. Hatred was forcing him to discover, deep
down within him, new reserves of strength and equili-
brium.

This was what the experts had wanted. There were
several ways of achieving the same result. Some trainees
had survived the tests, centuries earlier, with nothing but
their enthusiasm for new worlds to support them.

In others, fear alone had acted, forcing them to find
within themselves defenses against it.

But the paths of darkness had led Algan to other
regions, around other bends. Had the experts been able to
read Jerg Algan's mind they might have felt less compla-
cent.

For at the very moment when he reached the core of
his being, hatred took over every ounce of his energy. His
nerves obeyed. His glands poured out complex secretions
into his veins.

At about the thirty-sixth minute he rediscovered himself
through his hatred. During the last five minutes he had
learned more about man and the universe than he had
during the preceding thirty-two years of his life.

He relaxed, allowed himself to fall. He suddenly came
out of the night.

When they rushed forward to help him as he staggered
from the great chair, they neglected to notice, just before
he fainted, the cold glint in his eyes.

The big armchair was the end-all of the art of illusion. Its electrodes took the place of the real world and could conjure up any imaginable grotesque or terrifying universe. Simplified versions of the chair were in use in auditoriums on some of the planets. On others, or sometimes on the same ones, the chairs became instruments of torture. They were used in all ports to test pilots and pioneers.

The chair was the result of three centuries of research on the nervous system. It made possible the control of every fiber, the linking or unlinking of a multitude of synapses. For complex nervous systems it was the sole existing treatment—that is, if the patient survived.

The chair constituted a universe in itself. There was a legend that the great Tulgar himself, who had built the first chair according to specifications made ten centuries earlier by his brilliant precursor Bergier, had committed suicide after trying his creation because he had found no other use for it except as a potential paradise or hell, both of which were inextricably entwined. Scarcely one century later, at the beginning of the conquest, someone remembered Tulgar; the chair which was the repository of all the wonders and horrors of the universe was found in the attic of a university.

Algan learned to fall, without flinching, into darkest night and still retain his awareness of the immensity of space.

Hatred was his lifeline. Because at first he did not know on whom to concentrate it, the feeling was a rough and shapeless, but vital one. Then he began to hate the port, that alien element which had been imposed on the Old Planet, and to think up, in a cool detached manner, the means of destroying it. But his cold anger was soon transferred to those who had built the port. It was during his second week of training, when he was feeling as though he had spent at least ten years in the subterranean regions of the Stellar Port, that he decided to destroy the central government.

Conquering stars and strange new worlds meant nothing to him. All he knew was that it had taken brute force to

detach him from the Earth. He decided to become the cog
that would slowly and methodically cause the breakdown
of the great human machinery that had been set up to
conquer the stars.

After he had learned to control the night and his de-
scent into it, he was sent off alone on worlds that were either hostile or different from anything he had ever known.
One day, he flew down and hovered over an enormous
shiny surface. He suddenly found himself stretched out on
the ground, unable to move. He knew he had to get up and
walk, but he was glued to a huge metal sphere larger than
the Earth. The heavy black sky, studded with stars, seemed
to crush him.

Painfully he got up on his knees. The air was dry and
icy, so dry and icy that it burned and tore his lungs.

Algan knew he had to walk in a given direction, but he
couldn't even move, let alone take a step. He was engulfed, drowned in fear, yet he could see nothing anywhere
that would account for the terror that paralyzed him.

The fear was within him. He was alone. He had never
before been afraid of solitude. He had traveled, alone,
across enormous distances on the oceans and continents of
the Earth. But that solitude was nothing compared to
what he was experiencing here.

He had learned, as the technicians who were in charge
of his training had intended he should, that the only survival possible in a strange world is group survival; death
for a single individual was inevitable.

But the lesson did not stop there. One had to learn to
survive alone, if one happened to stray off, temporarily,
from the rest of an expedition.

He started to creep along the icy surface. Some unknown force was spurring him toward a particular point
on the horizon. Trying to slow the rhythm of his breathing, he dragged himself forward along a few hundred
yards. Just then the entire surface of the planet tipped and
he was thrown forward, slipping faster and faster. His
hands feverishly sought something to cling to, but there
was nothing. He finally let himself slide along the smooth
plain, his hands in front ready to break a possible shock.

His fall accelerated. He saw the sky slowly change and the color of the plain grow lighter. The polished steely surface slowly became luminous. At the same time an enormous red sun rose on the clear horizon.

He knew he was falling toward that sun and that nothing could save him. The red sun seemed glued to the horizon. But just as Algan was drawing near, it climbed up and floated amid the stars, eclipsing the nearer ones, devouring the night.

Then the wind bore him off.

He was blown about like a straw by the gentle breeze that brushed the polished plain which was now growing red. Then a storm blew up and began to roar. He was lifted up into the air, helpless to control his course. He flew over the surface of the planet and had the impression it was flying past him at a dizzying speed. He saw a huge dark shape looming up on the plain, which appeared to be sending out shapeless tentacles toward him. He tried to cry out, but he had no breath left.

Then he realized that it was only his shadow, that he was passing under the giant red sun.

He was climbing. The storm bore him so high that he could see the entire planet; it was like a disk unbelievably large and concave, rather like the inside of a bowl. Then the wind suddenly died down. He could no longer breathe. He was at the same height as the stars and as his lungs collapsed, his heart gave out, his blood ebbed away; he knew that he was going to die as he flew over the frontiers of emptiness.

He made an effort. He tried to escape from that deadly balance. But his reflexes were gone; his mind was blank.

He rolled up into a ball, then violently stretched. He began to hate the red sun which had started to disappear behind the steel disk. And suddenly he plunged.

Algan had the impression of a closed trap. He could get back to the ground and crawl again and rediscover the red sun and be swept up by another cyclone, or by the same one on its way back. He began to fume with rage as he fell uncontrollably, damning the chair, the technicians, the port, the Earth and Dark, space, interstellar ships and, above all, the central government of Betelgeuse.

I'm nothing but a toy, a puppet, he said to himself. *I'll get the one who is holding the strings.*

There was nothing here for him to attack or destroy. But behind that hostile and cold facade of the universe someone was watching.

Someone who was laughing at his vain efforts.

Someone who made fun of men.

Someone who set the stage.

I'll get him, Algan said to himself. He noticed that he did not want to die.

Not in this desolate icy world. Not before he had destroyed this odious setup.

He found himself again on the icy surface, in darkness. The red sun had disappeared.

He began to crawl with a cold determination. He saw another sunrise, this one blue, surrounded by fog and circled by three smaller revolving suns whose colors changed with their positions.

A shadow loomed up on the horizon and slowly grew bigger.

He crept along faster. Was it a new stage set? A new trap? He broke out in a fine sweat. The ground seemed to warm up, the closer he came to the shadow. The steel grip which had clutched him loosened. He got up on his knees and slowly stood up. Stretching to his full height, he scanned the horizon, then turned around. The multiple shadow cast by his body, from the light of the midget sun and from its satellites, was the only interruption on the plain.

He began to run.

There was a city stretching out the edge of this world. A dream city. Its crystal towers dominated the steel plain; its high walls looked like luminous cliffs defying cold and the night of the desert. Ancient bridges connected the palaces which stood silhouetted against the black background of emptiness.

There were people inside, a whole population ready to welcome him and celebrate his arrival. Flags were flying from turrets. Festival music rang in his ears.

He began to shout and dance with the intention of alerting the watchman on the turrets of his presence. He stopped, expecting some sound: the crack of a pistol shot, the noise of a rocket opening in the sky.

Nothing. No one.

He began to run again. He was filled with a terrifying premonition. There loomed before him, under the cold light of the blue sun, the high bronze gates of the city. A blurred memory stirred within him. These gates were not unknown to him. The high wall was very near. He hurled himself against the huge doors which were ten times his height, and he beat on them steadily. The bronze gates resounded like great gongs.

No one. Nothing.

He pushed forward with all his might; surprisingly, the huge bronze doors slowly gave. He slipped through the crack he had made.

I've done it, he thought. *I've done it*.

He walked out in the shadow of the huge porch, then continued forward under the cold light of the blue sun, onto a huge deserted square enclosed by tall white polished walls. Opposite him were the high towers and a building so tall that it seemed to touch the stars.

Silence.

I've seen this before, he thought.

He stepped onto the middle of the square and looked all around. No one.

He began to laugh. He remembered. He had come back to the port from which he had set forth thousands of years ago and now everyone had died, the planet was dead and so were the stars. He would never leave the Earth. He was the last man on a cold planet.

Algan wiped the sweat from his forehead. He dropped to the ground, stretched out on his back, and looked at the blue sun and its satellites that were slowly shrinking in the sky.

It isn't true, he thought, and he closed his eyes, trying to find the dark and to fall into a starless space. In a way, he found a certain peace. He began to hate, coldly and methodically, and filled space with a myriad stars of hatred.

He felt better.

It was then that they woke him up.

The training program in the underground of the Stellar Port lasted five weeks. Algan lived alone the entire time as part of the training. He saw only the shadows of the technicians, who never spoke a word to him. Thanks to his reflexes, he managed to survive a species of mental night, haunted by the adventures he had in the chair: he was parachuted onto water planets and swam for hours on the surface of oceans saltier than those of the Earth; dragged himself through countless marshes; climbed sharp cliffs; crossed chasms; balanced on an almost invisible cord; jumped down from terrifyingly high peaks; was slowly swallowed up by moving sands; was blinded by burning suns; was smothered by storms; was asphyxiated by clouds of red sand; was crushed by spongy soft rocks that were sickening to the touch.

Then, toward the end of the fifth week, when the look in his eyes had hardened, their sockets deepened and the experience of ten years in space could be read in his emaciated features, he was allowed to come up to the surface.

It was only then that he discovered the Stellar Port. He lived in the huge building under the control tower that challenged space with its antennas. He roamed at will among the rockets, questioned pilots, sailors, and explorers. He gradually discovered what mark man had made among the stars.

The stars stored up incalculable wealth and almost infinite sources of power. They were heaven and hell combined, just as the chair had hinted. But, inhuman though they were, the stars were the universe, a glittering irresistible prize which men repeatedly tried to ensnare in the web of their voyages.

The names of the ships evoked foreign lands. Their shapes varied according to whether they came from the edges of the Galaxy or from its more central regions. Only the black outmoded ships of Betelgeuse remained unchanged; their powerful engines still enabled them to give chase to any stellar craft or to reach any inhabited world.

The contents of the storehouses came from all the corners of the Galaxy. The scent of zotl roots embalmed one area of the port while piles of Aldragor's weightless furs, quivering in the lightest breeze, filled another area. There were transparent cages filled with splendid or repellent animals awaiting their fate: giant spiders with bodies as shiny and pink as a human skull, vampires with red wings, amphibians from Zuna in shapes that were changeable and vaguely nauseating, animated stones from Alzol, which sparkled like braziers enclosed in a block of changeable glass.

Algan learned to tell where the sailors came from by their accents, the color of their skin, the shape of their skulls, the color of their eyes. He soon learned to tell a ship's year and model from its hull. Some of the hulls had been built on the Earth itself, four centuries earlier, at the beginning of the conquest. They were still plowing the cold currents of space.

Algan spent days on end walking along the lookouts on the battlements, discovering anew the old city as it looked from the Stellar Port. It seemed oddly distant, alien. He felt almost as though he had just landed from a ship and was seeing, for the first time, the teeming city with its apartment houses stacked close together and its narrow, sordid little streets. He knew he would not go down into the city again before his departure. The Stellar Port was as remote and distant as a ship; he might just as well have already left the Earth. The Stellar Port was like a foreign growth on the city, a meteor from the sky, deeply bedded in the planet but barely tolerated. Algan knew he belonged to the old city and looked upon himself as a prisoner of the port. It was not a pleasant impression.

"You're a strange man," the psychologist told Algan.

They were both looking down from the top of the giant tower at the constant movement in the port: the arrivals and departures of the throbbing little cargo ships which kept communications open with the other cities of the Earth and made possible the launching of heavy rockets.

"I suppose there were a great many men like you when the conquest started. People who liked their own planet and who saw in the conquest of space only an infinite extension of their own world. The problem is finding out what our civilization can do with people like you."

"I did not ask it to do anything with me," Algan said dully.

"I know that," replied the psychologist.

He looked up and scanned the heavy clouds in the sky. "But your views are not very important. Men make up a large body in space. Do you think the opinion of one small cell is of any importance?"

With a faraway look he considered the irregular piles of the old city.

"Your thinking is outdated," said the psychologist. "It may once have been valid. I don't know. But man is now faced with problems he never had before. Old ways of thinking must go."

He turned his light, cold eyes on Algan. His bald pate shone.

"A certain amount of freedom, a certain amount of power. That's an equation. And the solution is a new way of thinking. It is starting, you know, in all the ports of the Galaxy, in the heart of the remotest jungles, on board the shabbiest ships. It is no longer a product of time or of history; it is the result of little skirmishes against space and of a great interdependence of men, beyond time and space, from one end to the other of the inhabited portions of the Galaxy. A ship left a distant planet three years ago in relative time, fifty years in Earth time, and its movement may well determine your fate even though its trajectory was determined before your birth. One is powerless in the face of these things. Probably the first medusae which were agglutinated to form a multicellular body felt the way you do, although on a different scale; they must have felt desperately diminished, imprisoned. But the process was their only means of becoming less dependent upon their environment and of conquering oceans, then the land, and finally of becoming what we are. If you'd been a medusa you would probably have tried to kill one of those multiple beings. I am assuming that right now you'd like nothing better than to destroy this embryo humanity, still rough-hewn, still in the process of growing. That's why you interest me. I don't expect to win you over. But you belong to a species that is rare nowadays: a rebel. There are perhaps a few million rebels in this world; we send them out as pioneers into space. There was a time when your kind ruled this world. It was a time of poverty and wars. But it was also a period of glory. Our glory is different. It is the result of the effort of trillions of men, millions of sailors, thousands of scientists. Do you know what is being done right now in Betelgeuse? The editing of a galactic encyclopedia. It is something like a memoir of the entire Galaxy, which will be added to as more discoveries are made. . . . Can your mind encompass such an undertaking?"

"Leave me alone," said Algan.

Toward the end of his second week of freedom, he ventured into the high tower that dominated the port. Doors opened readily for him. The electronic eyes that operated them must have been given his description and that of all the other explorers so that they could go about in the port, wherever they wanted, learning its layout, which was roughly the same as that of all the other ports of the explored areas of the Galaxy. Algan seldom ran into his future companions. He avoided them as much as possible. Most of them were the sort to whom he would never have spoken in Dark unless armed with a loaded weapon at the ready. However, here they seemed inoffensive and disoriented, even more lost than Algan. They spent day after day in their own quarters, playing and quarreling, but not daring to fight. They would feel more at ease in the new worlds, axes in their hands and weapons in their belts, fighting a defined and visible enemy.

As he slowly climbed long inclined planes, propelled by the gentle push of the anti-gravity fields, borne along on an invisible and insubstantial platform, Algan could understand the attraction that places like Dark had for the Galaxy. It was a carefully tended human reserve, an artificial one perhaps, from which, when the need arose, the government of Betelgeuse drew men accustomed to living like wolves and settled them in little known worlds. Algan was, willy-nilly, nothing more than a cell in the Galaxy. His hatred was strengthened by this thought even as he was busy admiring the huge passages that led to the top of the great dungeon.

Viewed from the inside, the top of the tower seemed to float in space. Its walls were huge windows that looked out on the sky and on the hustle-bustle of the port, but the windows made of one-way glass imprisoned the light. Seen from the outside, the tower looked like an opaque structure without openings that might have been massively carved out of a mountain, then dropped on the ground. From the inside, it looked like a fragile glass and microcrystal metal construction, as soft to the touch as old velvet. But it must have been incredibly strong. A lost spaceship crashing into it would probably not have shaken it.

The control centers of the Stellar Port, which were at the top of the tower, directed the commercial traffic and coordinated the activities of the black astroships of Betelgeuse.

Algan went through a door that led to the transmitting station of the tower. Even before the partition had opened, he knew what he would see. Although it was his first visit to this section of the port, he unerringly found his way through the labyrinths of corridors and wells. He knew that any information he might need had been hypnotically engraved in the lower levels of his memory. It was always information of a practical nature. He did not know how the gates and the awesome installations that he had discovered worked, but he knew how to use them. The technicians who had taught his subconscious cared little whether he understood. All that mattered to them was that he fulfill certain requirements.

Algan had often wondered how many technicians themselves understood the working of the port. Perhaps no one on Earth understood. Perhaps they were secrets jealously guarded by Betelgeuse, and perhaps that was one explanation for the surprising unity of the human Galaxy beyond the oceans of space and the abyss of time.

The transmitting station was in the shape of a well whose walls were covered with small alveoli connected by a spiral staircase leading right up to the topmost dome. Each alveolus was staffed by a technician who manned the instruments, received and transmitted messages. All the voices from distant space could be heard. Beyond the Galaxy of stars, beyond the Galaxy of ships and men

there existed another stellar complex made up of separate
sounds: scattered information, signals blinking in space,
breaths, voices, murmurs.

These voices assailed him as he wound his way up the
staircase and passed by the alveoli one by one. The voices
were toneless, deep, tense, disembodied, expressive of
some acute suffering undergone beyond space and time;
they were the voices of larvae crawling along the lowest
strata of emptiness, hopelessly imploring some unimaginable salvation. They were the voices of another age in time,
of another world.

As he looked at the calm faces of the technicians, Algan tried not to hear those distant, tortured, distorted,
heavily vibrant voices: those harsh cries, those metallic
shrieks, those sinister hisses.

Words.

He could understand words. They told the position of
ships; they spoke of new planets situated at ten years of
Earth travel time, of formulas, of names, of dates now
meaningless; they gave arid, meticulous reports; they re-
ported calls for help that had been moaned far from any
human ear—all this mangled, diluted in time.

Time.

Time which was quick here and slow there, depending
upon the movement of the ships, of the planets. Time,
variable and misleading, the destroyer of information;
time, which could transform a warm human voice into an
almost toneless, shapeless sound barely audible against the
crackling background of the music of the spheres; that song
of exploding stars, that grinding of particles, projected by
another Galaxy, which continued their unending voyage
through emptiness, setting antennas in motion once every
million years.

Time.

Every planet, spaceship, star, fragment of the universe
possessed its own time and completed its orbit at its own
speed. The transradio, alone, denied time by challenging
space. It made possible the transmission of infinitesimal
quantities of energy by passing through complex dimensions which shortened the longest paths of the universe but
which would not have allowed the passage of spaceships,

nor even the smallest grain of matter, without profoundly altering them.

The transradio worked on the same principle as interstellar ships but much more roughly.

Spaceships could not travel faster than light, but there were shorter paths in space than those uncovered by optical telescopes. These plunged into the very heart of the universe, following the shortest curves, and could shorten to one year a trip that could have taken one century. But there was one drawback. The more the path was shortened, the worse was the quality of the transmission. The more complex the dimension chosen for the transference, the more the ship was altered upon arrival, sometimes to the point of annihilation. Therefore, scientists had sharply defined the margin of security. The paths from one star to another, although shortened, still remained tremendously long. But these were no problems to the transradio. It could follow a line in space which reduced distances to almost nothing. It mattered little if a message was modified on the way, if the information it contained was altered or cut down, so long as its content remained intelligible upon reception.

In this way, the transradio could connect different kinds of time, contradictory spans of time: Earth time, the velocity at which spaceships traveled, and the variable speeds of planets orbiting around their suns.

This explained the alteration of the voices. One minute spent on a ship that was approaching and decelerating was the equivalent of three minutes spent on the Earth, so the voice became slow, deep, spectral, drawn out like soft dough. The only messages that were comprehensible were those transmitted from a point in the universe which was moving at a speed plainly comparable to that of the Earth. But there were often considerable differences, especially in the case of the fast spaceships which traveled at almost the speed of light. Then a single word could be drawn out for one whole hour, the movement of distant, almost unimaginable lips was slowed down to a virtual stop. At times it took a week, or a month, for information to reach its destination. Codes were devised to avoid these inconveniences. The transmitting ship could record its message and send it into space via transradio at an accelerated rate of speed. And if this method turned out to be inadequate for Earth transmission, there were machines that were attuned to the grunting of human voices and, after a long session of listening, turned them into normal voices, comprehensible to a human.

Time.

With each step he took in the port, Algan came upon the mark of time. And he began to suspect that man was starting to colonize time, as, slowly, he had colonized space.

As he climbed toward the tower dome that opened to the skies, he realized that in less than a month there would be no trace of him left on the Earth except as one of those deep, warped voices emanating from a ship.

CHAPTER III

Along the Paths of the Void

Algan closed his eyes and stretched. His fingers unconsciously clutched the arms of his chair. It was his first voyage into space and yet, without ever having landed on, nor even seen the moon, Mars, Venus, Saturn, or Jupiter, he was going to take a great leap into space, a leap that would take him to the stars. He looked over the readyroom. There was nothing remarkable about it: there were only rows of chairs in which the explorers sat, pale-faced and drawn. They ignored one another.

Algan turned his head and examined his neighbor, a redheaded young man with square shoulders and a normally suntanned complexion which, for the moment, was livid. He was muttering something. Perhaps a prayer?

The shadow of the massive high tower was thrown on the large screen that was clear as glass. A voice intoned numbers and letters. It was a calm, cold voice, somewhat bored by this tedious work, that enunciated syllables with a touch of preciousness. It was the last voice from the Earth that Algan was to hear for a long time.

He was surprised that he was not paying more attention to this fact. Then he realized he was quivering with suppressed excitement. It was, after all, a departure. And this one was no different from others he had made in hydroplanes leaving the last ports of the Earth to plow the oceans.

Perhaps, after all, he would like the worlds he was going to discover.

But he knew he would never feel about them as the

Galactians did, nor even the people of Betelgeuse. The Galactians looked down on them. One world was much the same as another and all epochs were the same. The only things they considered important were the space they occupied on Earth, the amount of air they breathed, and the seconds during which they lived. As for the people of Betelgeuse, they looked upon these worlds in a purely proprietary, manner, their only interest being to get everything they could out of lands they would never visit. They all denied, systematically, the immensity of space. For them, space was only a series of problems to be solved, one by one.

A red light went on over the screen. Then the outline of the high tower became blurred and darkened. The light went out. There was no vibration, no dull and prolonged throbbing, none of the things Jerg had, in his ignorance, anticipated: no sudden crushing into a chair that had abruptly become hard, no wailing of engine nozzles, no grinding of metal. There was only another voice enunciating numbers and words, carefully mounting syllables and seemingly bored by this monotonous work.

Nothing. They were on their way. On the screen, stars trembled. Then, after they had crossed the last limits of the atmosphere, they merely shone, immobile, with a steady light unlike their apparent twinkling from the Earth. They were on their way.

Algan got up from his chair. He went cautiously down the passage, a prey to an indescribable fear brought on by the lessening by one-third of the force of gravity he had been used to during his thirty-two years on the Earth. The gravity which was the same as that of all the ships that plowed the Galaxy would be maintained during the entire trip, but the fear inside him would diminish.

He went up to the big screen. Then he turned around and looked at the astronauts as the ship sailed through space at a speed steadily increasing outside the solar system, outside the orbit of Pluto, toward their faraway destination, and said:

"Which star are we headed for?"

They looked at him, apparently dazed, without replying.

Algan sat down and scanned the faces of the three men
who were with him in the cold, nickel-plated room: Paine,
an old space navigator, with a pale, deeply lined face; Sarlan, the redheaded young man who had been his neighbor
at takeoff; a short, squat, pop-eyed man with a thick
neck whose name Algan did not know. They were not a
bad-looking group. They were conscientiously trying to
imitate Paine's gestures and, as a start, tried to keep their
eyes off the screen which showed a black sky on which
only a few stars were visible.

"Which star are we headed for?" asked Algan.

Paine began to laugh.

"Worried, already, Jerg? You've heard too many stories
about monsters on distant planets. In a year or two you'll
complain about not having seen enough of them."

"What difference do you think it will make to us?" said
Sarlan in a bored voice. "One world or another. At the
point we've reached . . ."

The short, stocky man said nothing.

"We're headed for the middle of the Galaxy," said
Paine. "That's where there's the greatest concentration of
worlds in space. That's where our best bet is for finding
one suitable for humans."

"Let's have something to drink," said Sarlan in an un-
steady voice.

Paine opened a cupboard and took out a bottle and
glasses.

"To our departure," said Algan.

They drank in silence, avoiding one another's eyes.
Their eyes were fixed on the shiny metallic surfaces of the
walls. They looked somewhat uneasy.

Then Paine gave a small smile.

"You're not going to live in this cage all the time."

He ran his finger over some knobs. The light suddenly
went out. One of them dropped a glass and it bounced
with an echo on the flexible floor. Algan backed up until
he could feel the reassuring cold wall. He put his hands
out, ready to ward off an attack. His pupils dilated in an
effort to catch the slightest ray of light. But he was
floating in total darkness, in a silence punctuated only by

the whistling breath of his companions. He remembered old reflexes and fears and ways to overcome them.

Then the light came on again, at first creeping hesitantly along the cold end of the spectrum, then gradually increasing as it outlined the quivering contours of shadows, then bodies, then the metal clasps and buckles of their space clothes; it finally shone on the light in their eyes.

They could feel a strong breeze. They were waking up in an immense forest. Trees, centuries old, with emerald green leaves, swayed to the rhythm of the wind that blew around and over them. Somewhere in the bushes flowed an invisible spring.

Algan turned around. His hands felt the invisible surface of the wall. They were prisoners in an indiscernible cage and that forest which stretched out beyond imagination was illusory, unreal.

"So what they tell us about ships is true," he said. "Ships are magic places."

"Don't be afraid," said Paine. He was grinning as he leaned down and looked for the glass. His fingers closed over the goblet through tufts of grass.

"Don't be afraid," repeated Paine. "It's only a trick. You weren't warned so that the surprise would be greater, but it's only a trick. Just see what man can make out of a cold bare cabin. The sea, mountains, depths, and heights are within reach."

During the first years of space exploration astronauts would go mad from boredom and montony. Then psychologists devised total, perfect illusion: the transformation of the world into a series of stage settings, into a game. It was possible to plunge amid the stars or walk between ruined columns of palaces that had died thousands of centuries before on other worlds. As long as the trip lasted, you were a god. But you got used to it. You would look upon these ghosts of trees or waves only as a necessary antidote to claustrophobia. Man was born under open skies and no matter what he did, the immensity of those spaces weighed more heavily on him than a leaden cage. He could not escape empty skies for long. They stayed with him.

Empty illusion, thought Algan as his hands felt the cold

surface of the walls. *Empty illusions for undiscerning eyes.*
He remembered the old forests of the Earth and the long
hunts, the weariness that would creep up his cramped
limbs as he waited for his quarry, the wild chases, and the
feel of icy torrents on his shivering skin.

They sat on a mossy bench, old pewter tankards in their
hands. They were in a dream, actors in a dream of their
own, one that was drawn out for the length of the trip—
months—as the ship went through space in search of new
planets.

"What star are we headed for?" Algan asked for the
third time.

"The young stallion is already champing at the bit," said
Paine, laughing. "Well, I've already told you we were
heading for the center of the Galaxy. But our first stop
will be Ulcinor, one of the Puritan Planets. If any of you
wants to stay, I imagine it can be arranged. But it's seldom that anyone decides to do so after a few days spent
on one of those hellish worlds. You'll see why."

"And then?" asked Algan.

"Don't be in such a hurry. The worlds to which we're
going have no names as yet; only numbers. I don't even
know them. Maybe they'll be named after you, Algan, if
you're lucky enough to be killed during the trip. Algan
wouldn't sound too bad. But there's plenty of time. Right
now we have nothing to do except tell each other stories
or read or smoke to while away the time. After you've
visited a few inhospitable worlds you'll wish that these moments could have lasted a little longer."

Algan got up and took a turn around the room. He
could distinctly hear the sand squeak under his boots. The
forest disappeared near the entrance and he could see the
door, but if he moved off a few steps all he could see was
the wide expanse of trees.

He stretched out on the grass, closed his eyes, and felt
the warm rays of an illusory sun caress his skin, but his
hands slipped on the smooth surface of the ground.

"Why are we going after these impossible worlds?" he
asked dreamily.

His words seemed to him to dissolve in the silence. The
others were listening to him silently. He went on.

"We're being sacrificed for many reasons. What good will it do? Isn't there room enough, in the worlds that have already been conquered, for everybody, for a long time to come?"

There was something in their silence that he did not like, a shade of distrust, a faint smell of fear. It was a question that ought not to have been asked. He knew it and he raised his voice on the last words.

"It's Betelgeuse that decides," Paine finally said. "But you mustn't say things like that, son; it won't do."

"I want to know," said Algan. "I just want to know. I want to be sure that what I do will be of use to someone or to something."

"What difference does it make? You're asked to do something, do it! Is there ever anything in life that is of any use? Don't ask so many questions. It's a bad habit acquired on the old planets."

Paine was looking at Algan without a trace of impatience; his pale eyes looked empty, barely friendly. Algan wondered if there was anything behind those eyes except an absence of worry, an arid serenity, a slow erosion caused by time and the stars. He looked into Sarlan's eyes. The young man seemed frightened, but in his expression there lurked a tinge of admiration for Algan. Algan stretched his legs on the moss.

"It doesn't really matter," he said calmly. He was thinking of Betelgeuse, of that formidable and discreet government that spun the destiny of the stars and time.

Each new attempt to straighten out the tangle of space had only served to highlight its infinite complexity. With abstract and simple spaces as a starting point men gradually, in the course of ages, went on to geometric concepts that were increasingly difficult to formulate. One of the basic tenets of the idea of space was the geodesic line, that line which, in a given space, was the shortest path between two points. But real space was a multiple entity which postulated a large number, if not an infinity, of geodesics. Thus as the legendary Bergier discovered even before the conquest had begun, in order to connect two points in space one could plot several paths which in their own way

were the shortest, in the sense that each one allowed only
a predetermined amount of information to pass. This simply meant that, though they had no relation to physical reality, some of the paths were shorter than others. However, that shortcut might be offset by a more pronounced
alteration of the body or the message traveling along that
path. Certain geodesics, although seemingly ideal at first
glance, were therefore unusable for ships because, at the
start of the trip, the ships would undergo alterations fatal
to their crews.

The first ships just followed the paths of light at a speed
appreciably slower than that of light rays. Voyages in
those days were almost interminably drawn out and the
temporal distortion was almost nil, so accidents were rare.

Then there followed rapid progress. On the one hand,
the speed of ships increased to almost that of light, which
increased the time warp; as a counterbalance, a general
theory of geodesics was formulated at the same time as
the invention of the mathematical instruments required to
calculate the laws of probability governing the alteration
of bodies and messages along these new paths.

New ships soon made use of the extraluminous paths.
The latest improvements of accelerator-meters made it
possible, at the same time, to give up the old-fashioned
method of triangulating from the stellar sources of elec-
tromagnetic waves. A ship could at last determine with
satisfactory precision its absolute position by its calculated
coordinates, its speed, and the curve of its direction. A
certain number of unavoidable accidents were statistically
foreseeable, but within an acceptable margin. All the
same, these were negligible compared to the other risks
that the ship ran. Most of these risks came from the men
themselves. Homesickness and boredom, magnified by
fright and loneliness, gave rise to a nervousness that made
sharing close quarters unbearable. Psychologists worked
out acceptable conditions. Engineers tried to produce
them. A quick solution was generally found. Geniuses
were essential in a period of such feverish discoveries and
grandiose projects. They were found, trained, and put to
use. Some of them, pressed for time, did not hesitate to
use drugs which stimulated their mental efforts, but also

destroyed them after an alarmingly short lapse of time.
But it was a period of grandeur and enthusiasm.

The vest canvas uniting the stars was woven over the
years. Ships carrying astronauts left the cities of the old
planets and flocked to new worlds. New centers were
created. The human population increased phenomenally
within a few centuries, but the total number of humans
was still laughably small with respect to the number of
habitable worlds. There sprang up new myths about that
enormous space which was apparently impossible to popu-
late. New religions were practiced side by side with the
old ones. Historians and sociologists liked to emphasize the
absence of any serious conflict. Actually, the war that was
being waged was against another enemy: space.

Some utopias were successful; others failed. It was a
period of multiple and changing worlds. It was then that
the first meetings with the Puritan worlds were set up. It
was also at this time that the power of Betelgeuse became
first a determining one, then an undisputed one. It started
on an economical level, then became solely political, as
frontiers were pushed back by human expansion.

Certain plans were carried out successfully. Some attributed this evolution to the natural and general progress
of humanity; others attributed it to haphazard forces that
nonetheless had a statistically foreseeable result; still others attributed it to the schemes of one man or several men
operating behind the scenes.

This latter group, although they did not know it or in-
terpreted it in a wholly different context, were very nearly
right.

Jerg Algan opened his eyes. A fresh breeze caressed his
face. It was still night. Stars were shining in the sky and
two russet colored moons were slowly orbiting around one
another. The cries of animals could be heard in the distance. It was a long musical sound, a strangely comforting
one.

Jerg Algan raised himself up on an arm. The forest was
still. The moss looked damp although the morning dew
had not yet fallen.

There was no one near, not a trace of equipment, tents,

or men. He automatically felt for his weapon. It was not
there. Nor was his hunter's radiant in his belt.

"Where is the safari?" he grumbled.

He could barely remember what had happened. They
had spent all of the previous day wandering amid the ruins
that the man from Betelgeuse had been so eager to visit.
They had penetrated, but not very far, into the forbidden
section in order to hunt mutating animals, remains of the
last Earth war. They had finally settled for the night in a
clearing some distance from the native camp the smell of
which was unbearable.

Again Algan heard the distant howling. He had never
heard such an animal cry. There was something wrong in
this forest, something about the light. Were there really
two moons on the Earth? Or was it somewhere else? Scattered memories jostled each other in his mind.

He got up from his bunk and took a few steps. He noticed a man on another bunk and leaned down to look at
him, but he did not recognize him. He had never in his life
seen such a face, deeply lined and pale, so pale that it
seemed made of moonlight.

The moon. He remembered. There was only one moon
on the Earth. He was not on the Earth.

He was in the middle of space.

He shook the sleeping man. His memory turned up
names, faces.

"Where is the safari?" he shouted at the stranger.

Then he sat on the edge of the bunk and put his head in
his hands.

"Oh no, no," he said.

Something came up inside him, began to burn behind
his eyes. He knew it was anger, and something more.

"Come on, son, stop worrying," said Paine in a voice
thick with sleep. "We've been gone only two months and
we'll soon be on Ulcinor."

"I was . . . I was somewhere else," said Algan. "I
thought I hadn't left. I was in the deep forests of the
Earth."

"I know," said Paine. "I've seen others like you. For a
long time I was homesick for my town. It was a high,
proud city, perched on an alabaster column, in a world

you'll never see, and which I'll never return to, on the other side of the human Galaxy. I was free there, in a way that no one here can understand anymore. It doesn't matter. Worlds pass by, but men come and go, as the saying goes, you know. Come on, let's wake up Nogaro and go down to eat something."

Nogaro was a thin, brown, silent man with black eyes deeply set in a narrow face. His fingers were surprisingly long and his movements showed more agility than strength. But on the Earth or on any of the other planets, in ancient cities where the Psychological Police were not all-powerful, he could easily have passed as a dangerous man.

Nogaro shared Paine's and Algan's living quarters. He asked no questions, said nothing. Although he looked much younger, he appeared to know as much about space as did Paine.

The ship's technicians seemed to be superstitiously afraid of him and Algan knew that Nogaro had access to certain sections of the ship which were normally forbidden to astronauts.

While they were eating their rations in the refectory, Algan tried to get Paine to talk about Ulcinor, all the while watching Nogaro's reactions. Paine had only hinted at his knowledge of the Puritan Planets.

"You'll see when you get there," Paine answered once again. "All I can tell you is that their city is pretty dismal and that they wear curious masks. You'll get one when you leave the ship. But they're good tradesmen."

"I'd like to ask you a question, Paine," said Algan. "Has anyone ever escaped from the Psycho? Did anyone ever get back to his native planet?"

"What for?" asked Paine. "Only men from the old cities would ever get such an idea into their heads. Life in space has its ups and downs. But life on a planet isn't always a bed of roses either. Betelgeuse knows better than you what's good for you, isn't that right?"

"Are you quite sure?" said Nogaro.

"What did you say?" asked Paine, startled.

"I was asking you," said Nogaro, "if you're really sure

that Betelgeuse knows better than you what is good for you?"

Nogaro's voice was deep and muffled; it sounded remote, as though it had traveled over barriers and been carried by some strange echo along invisible cracks.

Algan leaned forward and stopped chewing in order to hear better.

"I don't know," said Paine slowly. "I'm just a sailor. I navigate through space and I grow older. Decisions are made over there, in Betelgeuse. I can't tell whether they're good for me or not. When I'm asked to explore a new planet, I go. I never know who the inhabitants will be nor what will grow there, but I do because I always have, I suppose, just like my father before me. We're not the kind of people who own land here and there and who feel rooted to their planet. We are free men and we leap from one world to another."

"Good," said Nogaro. His thin lips, drawn into a smile, revealed long teeth. "And you, Algan, what do you think? What do you think of Betelgeuse's policy?"

Algan laid his hands flat on the table and breathed deeply.

"I hate Betelgeuse," he said calmly but loudly enough to be heard at the neighboring tables. "I hate everything that comes from Betelgeuse and I don't trust its policies."

Heads turned toward him. Silence spread.

"May I ask why?" asked Nogaro.

"I come from old Dark," replied Algan, "and I'm not ashamed of it. I'm a man from the old cities and all I asked was to be left alone. What's the good of occupying new lands when we can't even settle the ones our ancestors plowed!"

The men at the tables closest to theirs were listening openly. Some looked at Algan with fear and disgust; others, less numerous, with a shade of admiration.

"It's a long story," said Nogaro. "I'll tell it to you some day but not now, not here. We must be powerful, Algan, extremely powerful, if we want to keep our empire. I, too, am a man from the old cities, Algan. I know how most people feel about you. Shall we join forces? We're both somewhat alien to this world, although in quite different ways. Perhaps our respective oddnesses will be complementary."

"OK," said Jerg Algan, and he remembered other friendships in a world that was now remote, which had been sealed in the barrooms of old Dark or on the hunting fields of the free Earth.

Nogaro had an astonishing mind, Algan thought soon after this exchange. He knew the history of the human Galaxy backward as well as an endless number of stories about each of the worlds of which it was made up. He gave the impression of having roamed through space since time immemorial. Unlike Paine, who kept telling the same stories, Nogaro could move easily from one story to another. The breadth of his experience was unbelievable. His only real enthusiasm seemed to be space and exploration but he spoke of the worlds as though they had been infinitesimal molecules that slid about within a restricted place. He was mad, Algan said to himself, mad from having looked too long at something too vast for man; but his madness was both grandiose and contagious. The problem that seemed to be haunting Nogaro was the problem of nonhuman races. He said that in the course of his wanderings he had met only races which differed little from the human species and that had attained only a primitive technological level. Yet some of their characteristics were strangely commonplace, so much so that he had decided to discover a race that was completely nonhuman, completely different. Old sailors' legends had led him to believe, he claimed, that such a race did exist. He would ply with questions anyone on board who had traveled along any unusual routes.

Nogaro taught Algan that the human Galaxy did not form a monolithic block and that the authority of Betelgeuse was not undisputed. There were rivalries aggravated by distance. But time was working for Betelgeuse. Rebels would disappear while the red star continued to shine in the sky. Betelgeuse had not only time on its side but knowledge as well.

Nogaro said that Betelgeuse was like a spider crouching in the middle of its web, watching the little drops of light

that were the stars, taking note of a tremor here, a quiver
there, and waiting, secure in its everlastingness and in its
strength; never pushing, but waiting, spinning threads to
catch rebel feet. And it was, said Nogaro, who had set
himself up as the interpreter of the rumors rife in the human Galaxy, an infallible spider because it was mechanical, soulless, immortal. It consisted of enormous machines
which, from their concrete strongholds surrounded by human servants, wrote the history of the planets according
to an inexorable logic. And men accepted their power because they were machines; cold, dispassionate, beyond the
reach of human ambitions and human imagination. Men
accepted them as they accepted the rivers and mountains
and space itself, even more readily because their own
breed had built them in times so remotely in the past that
they were becoming mythological.

Perhaps that was a tissue of lies, thought Algan; perhaps Betelgeuse was only a monstrous lie. Perhaps these
machines had existed only in the imagination of a dynasty
powerful enough to impose its rule for centuries, protected
by immense walls of space and by bottomless pits of time.

And where did Nogaro belong in this canvas, Algan
wondered. And how did he himself fit in? And what was
the role of all those who had conquered, explored, and
died, without ever knowing exactly what their function
was as they leaped from one square to another on this
cosmic chessboard?

What was Paine's place, with his naïveté; and Nogaro's,
with his cynicism, his cold, shrewd eyes, his calculating
silence, or his sharp tongue? What was Jerg Allen's place,
a man from old planets and old cities, from free, anarchic
worlds which looked back into the past rather than forward into the future, sifting, in ancient dust, glories that
were past instead of victories to come?

Was there a place for them? Were they not superfluous?
Were they simply nothing, just ashes in the great human
brazier that devoured space? Algan spent the last days of
the journey, before the landing on Ulcinor, in the ship's library, but he learned nothing from the films, tapes, or
books. Perhaps, after all, the world was simple, and therefore Algan hated it. Or perhaps it had a hidden face, a

secret, that had to be uncovered, which was reality, or a fragment of reality, and Algan hated it because it crushed the lives of men by means of myths.

Perhaps there was no one, from one end to the other of the human Galaxy, who any longer knew truth. Perhaps no one had ever known it. But Algan's mistrust, as he studied the films and the books and listened to the tapes, was that of the hunter uncovering a hidden trail, who has caught the scent of a quarry that is either stupid or dangerous. And he could find nothing as he went along, but he knew that animals and men can move softly without snapping twigs or stirring up the air.

Perhaps Nogaro was right. Maybe salvation would come from another race, a nonhuman, different race that could bring the weight of its experience. Or perhaps destruction would come from that other race. But the salvation and destruction of this civilization were intermingled in Algan's mind.

Algan's interest in the Puritan Planets grew as they approached Ulcinor. He knew little about them—just legends and gossip picked up in the dives of the old city of Dark, gloomy stories and a black reputation, but no precise facts. The abyss of space and time dulled the force of events. It was difficult to pass on traditions when everyone was isolated in time. And sailors disliked telling stories they considered dead. Sometimes explorers were more talkative, but they were seldom well-informed. Betelgeuse probably preferred this way. Betelgeuse intended to be the principal and, whenever possible, the only bond between the various universes.

Three hundred local years earlier, when explorers had first reached the planets which were to become the Puritan worlds, they had run into harsh and even hostile conditions which had molded their personalities. In addition, they had been the first genuine models of the Galactian civilization. Before their arrival, the conquest had been undertaken by men from the Earth who were still steeped in their own world, but the explorers of these new worlds were mature men who had spent most of their lives aboard slow spacecraft that traveled through the outer reaches of the Galaxy. They knew all about time warp,

they couldn't even conceive of a world ignorant of it, a
world that had only unchanging time. They felt like foreigners on the Earth, for they had been contemporaries of
people who had died, one or two centuries earlier. They
were looking for a new world in which time would have a
new value, in which men's lives would be less dependent
upon the lives of their contemporaries and more on the
lives of men to come. They discovered ten such worlds,
orbiting neighboring stars. They left their imprint upon
them, deeply enough to last for centuries.

Then other societies were created elsewhere in space.
The reason for the creation of the Puritan worlds became
meaningless, because the mentality of Earthlings had almost disappeared with the years. But the Puritan worlds,
bastions of a tradition, probably the only one in the human Galaxy except for that of Betelgeuse, survived, complete with their rigid organization and morality, their religion and strange customs which excluded foreigners. The
ports which Betelgeuse built or the Puritan Planets, like
the ones they had built on all the inhabited planets, were
soon abandoned. Engendered by space and its effects upon
man, the Puritan worlds soon began to distrust anything
new and worrisome that man might bring.

Distrust is perhaps a narrow form of wisdom. In any
event, the currents of space carried an embittered Jerg Algan to the shores of the Puritan worlds.

CHAPTER IV

The Puritan Planets

The name of the planet shone in letters of fire on the tall bronze gates of the Stellar Port: Ulcinor. It was an old-fashioned name, a light, musical one that trailed ancient myths, cloudy and disquieting memories, a name that rang out loud and clear but was also hemmed in by disturbing rumors.

As Algan went through the gates, he saw the suburbs; at first all he could see were the roofs through which narrow streets wound like narrow trickles. Then in the distance he could make out the colossal shadows of the new city. He was to be free for many long days, free to come and go on the planet, but not to leave it. He knew that the government of Betelgeuse was most reluctant to lose a new recruit; he also knew that he would doubtless prefer life on board stellar ships to that on Ulcinor, if even one-tenth of the legends told about the dismal Puritan worlds was correct.

Before entering the city he slipped his hands into long black gloves and covered his face with a dark mask. It was equipped with light filters for the nose and ears to allow the passage of sound, air, or smells; the mouth was covered; only the eyes and forehead were in the open.

Algan had been warned never to go without the mask. Going out barefaced was tantamount, for the Puritans of Ulcinor, to a crude insult, to a deliberate act of indecency; the penalty for violators was a heavy one, even if he was protected, as an explorer, by the all-powerful administration of Betelgeuse.

Algan roamed about the old streets through which no vehicle now traveled. Behind those monotonously white walls that had split and cracked under the extremes of heat and cold of countless seasons, he could only sense a larva-like activity. He liked that. It reminded him of the Earth. The Puritan worlds were among those most violently opposed to the Earth's way of life but he liked the idea of finding a history and a decadence comparable to those of old Dark.

He remembered what Nogaro had said to him before he left the ship: "The Puritans are so afraid of growing old that the weight of their fear instantly aged them." It was true; he understood it now and once more admired Nogaro's strange mind: the Puritans had wanted to create a deathless civilization. Rigidly conceived, from its very inception it had borne the weight of the curse: it was doomed to sclerosis.

However, as he went on, the streets began to exhibit more liveliness. The Puritans had started out as merchants and they had never forgotten it; they had been explorers ready to grab what they liked in new worlds if only to sell it on the rich planets. Consequently, all the goods necessary for trade in the human Galaxy could be found in their ports.

Algan soon came across men who were no longer furtive shadows, but were obviously important people, dressed in dark velvet, black or dark blue, depending upon their status, and whose masks gleamed with bright stones. Shops were full of luxury items, unostentatiously displayed: antique polished wood from Atlan, light silky furs from Aldragor, or the products of native crafts: brightly colored shawls, glass blocks enclosing multidimensional and kaleidoscopic views, bronze plaques engraved with hieroglyphics, crystals in strange colors and shapes, glass bees, giant lifelike insects with powerful stingers.

There were no limits to the wealth of the human Galaxy, and its best products were assembled here on Ulcinor.

Jerg Algan felt lonely as he leafed through old books written in an unknown language or felt the softness of a piece of fabric. He was lonely as he seldom had been on the Earth. For the first time in his life, he felt lost in the midst of a new, upsetting world, friendless, without even a guide to show him the way, to protect him. And he was not free.

He tossed the fabric back on the counter, to the annoyance of the shopkeeper whose greedy eyes glinted inside his mask. Greed was deemed a virtue on this planet where human feelings were classed as vices. The inhabitants of Ulcinor assiduously cultivated cupidity.

Under the pile of fabrics, painted canvases, and embossed leather books, Algan noticed an old chessboard. He swept the materials aside and examined it. The sixty-four squares seemed to be made of two kinds of wood, one blue as the night, the other rosy as a delicate complexion. There was nothing unusual so far. But each of the squares was finely engraved. These curious markings drew Algan's attention.

The precision of detail and freedom of design were remarkable. It was almost impossible to believe a human mind could have conceived them. They were not sufficiently plain to have been intended as a decoration, nor was there any indication that they bore any relation to the game of chess.

Yet they stirred up vague memories which intrigued him. He had heard about signs like these, on the Earth, that had something to do with a very old science or, more precisely, with a religion ... no, he remembered now, it had to do with a superstition called astrology. Some of the signs etched on the chessboard looked like certain of the symbols which had been used to designate parts of the sky and groups of stars at a time when men believed their fates were written in the firmament.

But the other signs did not look like anything that could have been imagined by a human mind. There were arabesques, some geometric in character, others consisting of interlacings of fantastic figures, but unrelated to any human endeavor. There was no apparent connection with chess. The whole thing was rather like one of those mystical squares occasionally wrought by painters or engravers of antiquity.

Algan lightly touched the chessboard. It may not have been wood for the material it was made of showed a finer grain than even the finest fibrous wood. But it was not an ordinary synthetic either because the play of light on the dark and light squares revealed an unusually complex chemical structure.

He was surprised at how small the chessboard was. His two hands could almost completely cover it.

His curiosity began to fade. He said to himself that it must have belonged to some spaceman who had strayed on the planet by chance. Nonetheless he beckoned to the shop owner, who came up eagerly. Nothing in the shop was his; the inhabitants of Ulcinor considered it immoral to sell anything owned by them, but, paradoxically, acquisitiveness was considered a duty.

"Where does this come from?" Algan asked casually.

"It's a very old chessboard," said the shopkeeper. His yellow eyes glistened. "Very old. Maybe a thousand years old. Maybe ten, maybe more. Interesting. Are you a collector?"

"How could it be ten thousand years old?" asked Algan. "The conquest of space is more recent than that. What makes you think that the chessboard is that old? Are you trying to cheat me?"

But as he said it he didn't really believe it. He knew that Puritan shopkeepers were thoroughly honest; they never claimed that their products were better than they actually were; only, at times, they just did not mention flaws.

"It's older than any of us," the shopkeeper said. He stroked his mask. "It's older than this city. Believe me. It's extremely interesting. No one knows its date. It could be worth a fortune. But I have to sell it. Business is bad."

"Really," said Algan, smiling. "How much are you asking for it?"

"Let's not discuss the price, sir. At least, not right now. We both love beautiful old things, don't we? Look at this chessboard. Can you tell me what it is made of? There are old legends. . . ."

"Tell me first where the pawns are; then you can tell me your old legends."

The shopkeeper threw him a suspicious look.

"The pawns?" he repeated. "There are no pawns. Not with this kind of chessboard. I thought you were an expert. Did you at least notice the designs on the board?"

"Then how is it played?"

"No one knows. I told you this chessboard is very old, undated. There is no one now who knows the rules of the game. Boards like this were around long before man learned to move pawns in sixty-four squares."

"Where did this one come from?"

"I don't know, sir. A spaceman brought it to me to sell one day. He came from the w rlds that are on the outermost edge of the human Galaxy. I don't quite know where he found the chessboard. He didn't tell me. But I know these boards are very old. Not very rare, sir; we've seen lots of them in Ulcinor. Not very rare, but very old. Long before man came."

"There were other civilizations in the Galaxy before that of man?"

The shopkeeper looked at him sadly.

"How can I answer you, sir? I don't know any more than you do. Explorers, among whom were my ancestors, as well as yours probably, discovered intelligent races here and there, human or otherwise, but never one that was wholly civilized or that succeeded in leaving its native planet. But I believe . . . I believe, sir, that we are not the first to go to certain planets. I believe that They are watching us. I believe that They are waiting for us. Maybe They made these chessboards."

"Who are They?" Algan asked curtly.

"Who knows? Who knows? Certainly not a poor Ulcinor shopkeeper who hasn't made three trips away from his planet. But there are tales, strange tales."

"What sort of tales?"

"Do I dare speak? These are not supposed to be mentioned. But I can see that you're a friend and that you would give me a good price for this old and valuable board."

"All right," said Algan.

"Then follow me," said the shopkeeper. Algan looked
around. An animated crowd pressed against the shop windows; noiseless, long black cars went down the streets. But
all this activity was carried out in such complete silence
that the atmosphere was sinister; the dark masks and
clothes only added to the general gloom.

Algan went through the low narrow doorway into the
back of the shop; it was nothing more than a narrow hov-
el in which were piled up unimaginable riches: furs of incredible warmth and quality, finely engraved metal ob-
jects.

The shopkeeper sat down on a pile of furs and mo-
tioned to Algan to sit in a tall leather armchair which
plainly had come from the Earth. The light was somewhat
dim, but Algan's eyes soon became accustomed to it and
his gaze roamed over the little shop.

"I see you like my place, sir," said the shopkeeper. "It
quite warms my heart."

He leaned over toward Algan, giving him a conspirato-
rial smile, and said:

"Do you like zotl?"

"It's a long time since I've had any," sighed Algan. "But
I thought that in the Puritan worlds . . . ?"

"Oh, one makes compromises, sir," said the shopkeeper.
"We have a saying: Facades count only for those who do
not go inside. It's a very old saying. Don't you like it?"

The shopkeeper took a zotl root from a shelf and slipped
it into a small zotl squeezer which looked like an inoffensive bit of statuary. He waited until the hard root had
lost its color and the juice had run all the way down. Then
he poured the amber liquid into tall silver goblets.

"Wait," he said. "Don't drink right away, I want to
show you something. I know that I can trust you."

His tone of voice had changed imperceptibly. It had become less obsequious, less commercial; it had become
more precise, more positive. The shopkeeper intended to
be obeyed and Algan wanted to know what he was leading
up to.

"Place the chessboard in your lap, sir; put your right
hand over the squares, like that, each finger in a square. It
doesn't matter which ones. Now listen to me:

"We see all kinds of people on a planet like Ulcinor and usually people trust us because we have the reputation of being incorruptible. Our customs are not alway properly appreciated, and our intolerance, albeit justified, is often held against us. However, on the whole, foreigners trust us, and believe me, that's pretty rare, in space. So they tell us things that even Betelgeuse, in its mighty pride, does not know.

"You don't like Betelgeuse, sir, don't try to tell me you do. I could tell right away from your clothes that you are an explorer and that you come from the Earth, and I know how Betelgeuse recruits explorers on the Earth, even if the central government doesn't boast about the methods. Well, we too have good reasons for disliking Betelgeuse.

"For three centuries now, our influence has been restricted to the worlds you call Puritan, even though there are countless uncolonized planets in space. Betelgeuse wants our men, but not our society. She's afraid of us and keeps us from expanding.

"So we listen carefully to the stories travelers tell us and we are always on the lookout for some secret that will give us a hold over Betelgeuse. Someday we'll find one. We know, for example, that in certain worlds there are ruins more ancient than man."

He stopped talking and his deep-set yellow eyes scanned Jerg Algan's expressionless face.

"You are not surprised?" he asked.

"I'd already heard something of the sort," said Algan.

"Could be; or perhaps you're good at hiding your feelings . . . ? Perhaps I ought not to have spoken so soon. Never mind. I know you hate Betelgeuse as much as we do.

"Now, listen. A number of expeditions have discovered and photographed colossal ruins on the planets bordering the human Galaxy. Unfortunately none of those expeditions has come back."

"An accident?" Algan asked. His voice betrayed none of his surprise.

"They just simply disappeared. Perhaps they were destroyed. That's what Betelgeuse thinks. Or perhaps they just left. That's what we think."

"Left?" said Algan.

"Just imagine those ruins as being some sort of a gateway to everything you can conceive; imagine that those expeditions set forth, trustingly, into new universes and that they were never able to get back."

"Absurd," said Algan.

"No doubt, no doubt," replied the shopkeeper. "But men did come back a couple of times. Oh, not straight back, and usually under different names. Betelgeuse never saw them again even though they had sworn loyalty to her years earlier. But we found them. They had something to sell and they offered it to us."

"What had happened to them?"

"Nothing. You mustn't think I'm trying to hide the truth from you, but nothing had ever happened to them. Their stories were, for the most part, surprisingly similar. They had been left behind by the main body of the expedition, usually to keep an eye on the campsite. But no one ever came back to relieve them. So then they fled, taking with them anything of value in the camp, sometimes after having taken a few snapshots.

"We have all those snapshots. Those ruins really do exist."

"They're too ancient," said Algan.

"Do you think so? After all, the expeditions did vanish."

"All right, but what connection can there be with this chessboard, and why are you telling me this?"

The shopkeeper's black silk mask creased so markedly that Algan could see he was smiling.

"Put your fingers on the board, sir, either hand, each finger on a square. Good. Now drink your zotl."

Algan lifted up his mask and slowly emptied his glass. He was racked with homesickness. He could remember the Earth and the shady barrooms of Dark and the imaginary land that the zotl conjured up. A gray desert under a low green sky, iridescent and changeable rocks. Distant and invisible suns vibrating like harp strings. But this time the zotl did not affect his ganglia and he neither heard colors nor saw sounds.

He felt as though he were on the chessboard and as though he were nothing but a pawn in a white square; he

could not see the edges of the board. He was rigid, perfectly still, his eyes fixed in space, his stiff arm holding the
glass. He was no longer himself. He was traveling on the
chessboard.

An irresistible force propelled him. Then the squares
around him began to change and grow larger. He could
see stars shining in the darkening sky; he flew briefly over
a green stretch, then went down vertically and landed
gently in tall undulating grass.

The grass reached up to his shoulders, but he forgot
about it as he looked around because, under that lavender
sky studded with a gigantic blue star, the black polished
walls of cyclopean ruins glistened.

It was a wall. But he started to shout. He saw it crack,
collapse, and then it crushed him. It was only a dream,
but he fluttered his eyelids. The wall was too big, too
smooth, too unbroken to have been made by humans; too
black also. It was not perfectly vertical, but clearly slanted, leaning over Algan's landing place. That was what
had made him think that the wall was collapsing.

Then Algan looked up toward the sky and tried to decide which sun it was, but he suddenly felt a weight at the
end of his arm. He blinked and saw the masked face of
the shopkeeper over him.

"What is it?" he said, even before putting the goblet down
on the table.

"How do I know? I wasn't with you," the shopkeeper
replied.

"You knew what was going to happen to me. You told
me to put my hand on the board. Zotl never sent me there
before."

"Probably not," said the shopkeeper. "Well, now you
know as much as I do. You can be sure that there really is
such a place, just as you saw it. Those walls have been falling, for thousands of years, toward the section of the
ground on which you were standing. Was the sun in the
sky blue, red, or still yellow?"

"It was a large blue star," said Algan.

"That's the most usual. You see, there are many factors
that affect these visions. The vegetation, for example, or
the color of the sky or the sun, but the walls never

change. These colossal fortresses appear in all the worlds that have some connection with this chessboard and with zotl. Heaven only knows what treasures they contain."

"Or what weapons," said Algan.

They were silent for a moment, then looked at one another.

"An hallucination," said Algan.

"Probably," said the shopkeeper, "an hallucination that kills."

Why did you never send out an expedition?"

"Because of Betelgeuse," said the shopkeeper. "Ships and technicians are only for Betelgeuse. You know how few men there are. But we've learned quite a lot anyway, as you can see. Yes, quite a lot."

"And now," said Algan somewhat uneasily, "Tell me why you've told me this."

The shopkeeper's eyes closed almost entirely.

"You were interested in the chessboard," he said. "I thought you were really interested; was I wrong?"

"No," admitted Algan, "but there must be another reason."

"We Puritans like to spin yarns," said the shopkeeper. "We also like to hear them. Imagine for a moment that you see something, or even only hear of something, of a large black slanted wall, for example. You may be sure we'd be so glad to know more that it would be worth a great deal to us to hear about it. A very great deal."

"I'm only an explorer," said Algan. He hesitated to say yes. He wasn't sure he could trust the shopkeeper and was afraid of a trap. "I don't even know where my first trip is going to be. I couldn't be of much help to you."

"Who knows?" said the shopkeeper. His eyelids were fluttering as though he were transmitting in Morse code a secret message to some invisible assistant. "Who knows? Perhaps tomorrow you will be traveling, free, among the stars. Whatever happens to you, don't forget us."

"I'll bear it in mind," said Algan. "And how much do you want for the chessboard?"

"Nothing," said the shopkeeper. His voice was heavy with regret, as though he were committing a sin too burdensome for his conscience, which was precisely the case.

"Nothing," he repeated. "It's a present."

"There is more to this than meets the eye," Jerg Algan said to himself as he walked through the streets.

Nogaro had been right on almost every score. The human Galaxy was not a monolithic bloc, but a kind of yeasty mass pulled in every direction by different ambitions. Perhaps one single shock would suffice to topple the power of Betelgeuse. The idea appealed to Jerg Algan.

But what really surprised him was the interest in nonhuman races that Nogaro and the shopkeeper had shown. This interest must have sprung from information that he, Algan, did not have. It could well be related to the instability of the power of Betelgeuse over the Galaxy, or to some intelligence that could endanger her. The Puritan worlds fully expected that the discovery of the black stone fortresses would give them victory over Betelgeuse. They probably knew more than the shopkeeper had been willing to tell Algan. But what was his, Jerg Algan's, role on this gigantic stage set, he wondered uneasily as his fingers ran over the smooth surface of the chessboard.

There was no immediate answer.

Each of the trails he mentally explored was a dead end.

Ulcinor was a planet peopled with shadows, tall black flames that sped along the streets.

The place was filled with black-masked figures in flowing capes that shielded their wearers from probing looks. The animation in the streets had something furtive about it, as though the inhabitants of Ulcinor, in striving to look like sexless ghosts, had ended up by acquiring the habits of timorous specters. The cars in the streets were long and black, and the windows on their outsides were mirrors that reflected passersby. They rolled by silently, smoothly, at a fast and steady speed. There was something funereal about them; even the chrome glistened somberly.

No one carried weapons. This surprised Algan, who had always seen the men in Dark wear all kinds of radiants in their belts. The sense of security here was such that no one would ever have thought that speed and skill in self-defense were necessary for survival.

Ulcinor was a world of enduring solid traditions. The Earth, too, had once had them, Algan knew, but now— and he realized for the first time with poignant certainty—it held only chaos and decomposition.

The new city surprised Algan. He saw now that Dark, despite its splendor, was nothing but a city from the past in the process of decay. Here the huge black and white buildings were taller and more majestic than those in Dark. There were towers stretching toward the sky that could have crushed, by their sheer weight, even the tower of the Stellar Port of the Earth.

But boredom and anxiety seemed to have taken over. It was a cold city, peopled with shadows that had forgotten their human destiny, who whispered to one another instead of speaking out, who ran silently in the shelter of walls. It was already a dead city, muffled in the shroud of its silence, just like the thousands of faces behind their masks.

The idea of the ancient Puritans had been that each man, confronting an immense but not inaccessible universe, was and ought to be quite alone, that he had to count only on himself or on the mathematical laws calculated to insure his protection or his survival. Spaceman could no longer be the man of a particular epoch or a particular world. He had to be detached from everything and be interchangeable. He had to be colorless, odorless, almost invisible, nearly inaccessible.

In the space of a few hundred years he had, in effect, achieved just that. At least in the Puritan worlds. One could leave Ulcinor, then come back a century later and find it unchanged. The streets were always the same, the black and white facades barely feeling the breath of time along their surfaces. The men behind their masks might have changed, but there was no way of telling.

Jerg Algan remembered the men and women of the Earth, their strong resonant voices, their brightly colored and occasionally original clothes. Here, he was able to recognize the women only from their long hair floating in the breeze and their slender figures. But their features, lips, and cheeks were hidden behind smooth unchanging masks and their supple bodies disappeared under the full, dark cloaks.

This was the world of the future, Jerg told himself as he stared at the bare, blind facades which on Earth would have had a wealth of light, windows, curtains half-opened like eyelids on the serene warmth of welcoming rooms. His hands in their long black gloves shook with anger. His lips quivered with anxiety and nervousness under his mask of featherweight silk.

Would space produce a different kind of future: one that had been engendered in worlds immemorially old or still to come?

No one knew, Jerg Algan thought, as he walked through the wide streets of Ulcinor, checking the length of his stride and trying to look like everybody else.

He felt a hand on his shoulder. He turned quickly and noiselessly. His hand instinctively reached for his belt. But there was no weapon there, no sheath.

"I gather that you are taking an interest in antiques and shopkeepers." Nogaro's voice, muffled but clear and slightly ironic, reached him.

"How do you know?" Algan replied curtly.

"Never mind. I hear all sorts of things. Have you seen the roofs of Ulcinor? Believe me, they're worth seeing. Come on. I want to have a talk with you. We'll be less likely to be disturbed up there."

Nogaro took Jerg Algan by the arm. They went through the gate of an enormous building and crossed a number of white rooms. There was a crowd of masked figures milling about. At the end of this corridor Algan saw an enormous spiral staircase that seemed to be revolving on itself. He realized, when they set foot on it, that it was an escalator.

Algan had never seen one like it on the Earth.

"Don't bother to tell me what the shopkeeper said to you," Nogaro said. "I know. I just want to warn you about a number of strange things that will certainly happen to you."

Jerg Algan looked at Nogaro.

"Do you think there's any truth in all that?" he asked. "Do you really think that there exists in space another, more ancient civilization than man's?"

"I'd like to feel sure about it," Nogaro replied evasively.

"The chessboard and the zotl?"

"I don't know any more than you do."

"Those lost expeditions?"

Everything the shopkeeper told you about is true except what he said about Betelgeuse. Betelgeuse knows, as much as the shopkeepers do, neither more, nor less; just as much. And Betelgeuse, just like the merchants, would like to know more. Perhaps she will learn it from you. Who knows?"

"I'm only a spaceman. I don't even know in what world I'll be living next year."

"Who knows?" repeated Nogaro. It seemed to Algan that he was smiling under his mask. "Perhaps tomorrow you'll travel, free, among the stars. Perhaps tomorrow you will be leading an expedition."

A point in Algan's mind froze.

"The shopkeeper has already told me that," he said slowly. "Now, you. It looks as though I'm the least informed about my own future."

"You could well be, my friend," Nogaro said in a tone of cold finality. "Betelgeuse and the shopkeepers are cooking up something for you."

Algan became pensive. The escalator had taken them up to the top of the building. He looked up and saw a transparent cupola above. Black dots which he identified as spaceships could be seen in the sky.

Nogaro went on: "Betelgeuse might let you use a high speed ship. Oh, just a small one. Just a simple launch that one man could handle alone. In that way you could get to the distant skies in which the black citadels are located. But, as Betelgeuse would prefer not to have this known, she could ask you to take over a ship by force in a Stellar Port—Ulcinor, for example. It's been done before. And it would be easy enough to do. You've no idea how careless the port authorities are. So, you'd set forth in that stolen ship, and after a long voyage of exploration you'd bring back some interesting data. You would then become the object of a long struggle for power between Betelgeuse and the Puritans. Do you see?"

"I'm beginning to," said Algan. "But why did they choose me? And why are the Puritans giving me information that will be useful to Betelgeuse if I leave?"

"This is where things begin to get complicated. As far as Betelgeuse and the Puritans are concerned, you're nothing but a pawn. But as soon as one side has chosen you, the other one will take an interest in you also. You'll probably never know which one did so first, but that doesn't matter.

"Let's assume that you're not just an ordinary spaceman, not even among those that come from the Earth. You're able to survive alone in a hostile environment. But in addition you hate both Betelgeuse and the Puritans. You hate the present-day world. You would like to find, somewhere in space, the means of destroying it. You'll try hard to find those means. That's enough. Betelgeuse and the Puritans hope to discover, through you, a means of destroying the power that worries them: for the Puritans, the central government; for Betelgeuse, the Ten Planets. The information given you by the shopkeeper is of no importance. Betelgeuse already has it. It was given to you for the sole purpose of allaying your suspicions."

They were now directly under the cupola. The city spread out before them, all around the Stellar Port, just like a game of black and white dominoes lined up in even rows along a flat table. An enormous black ship carrying the colors of Betelgeuse whirled, like a giant insect, around the Stellar Port. The sky, above the city, was covered with the white wake of ships taking off.

"So, space is not large enough for Betelgeuse and the Puritans to coexist," said Algan.

"No," whispered Nogaro, "or rather, it's too big and there are too few men to permit either of the two powers to share. Perhaps the situation would change if men were to find a powerful ally in the skies. But so far they have discovered, along the line of thinking races, only primitive types who may have been failures of History and Time."

"Who are you, anyway?" Jerg Algan asked. "How do you know all this? For whom are you working? For yourself?"

"No," said Nogaro. He looked away, toward the city. "All of this is interesting, but I think I ought to tell you that I represent Betelgeuse."

CHAPTER V

All the Stars in the Sky

All the stars in the world were shining in the Ulcinor
night, Algan thought, and it was virtually impossible to believe that beyond that haze of suns there existed other
clouds of fire and other orbiting and perhaps inhabited
worlds.

He had left his room noiselessly and was now on the
patrol path formed by the top of the thick walls that surrounded the Stellar Port. A radiant hung on his belt and
he was wearing an air pilot's uniform. From the high wall
he could look down on the city and the port esplanade.
The air was fresh, the sky clear. He could see the lights of
distant suburbs, miles from the center, shining like little islands of stars, like galaxies detached from the firmament
and squashed on the ground.

The port itself was only a kind of white desert surrounded by walls and bathed in light, darkened here and there
by the black outlines of ships headed toward the zenith.
One of these ships, one of the small fast going units of Betelgeuse's inspection service, was waiting for him.

It made a small slender shadow at the southernmost
points of the port, a thin black spindle with all its lights
out. This was Jerg Algan's destination.

He was about to play an odd sort of game: hijack the
ship, with the secret cooperation of the port patrol. He
was to take the aircraft, ostensibly pursued by the whole
of Betelgeuse's space force, to Glania, a tenth-rate, sparsely settled world, but with a brand-new Stellar Port. Glania
was only the first lap of his journey, but a necessary one.

Glania was at the very border of the human Galaxy, on the edge of the troublesome regions of the center of the Galaxy. And it was on Glania that one of the two or three survivors of the lost expeditions now lived.

Glania, an invisible planet in the starry sky.

Algan carefully went over the contents of his pockets. He was not supposed to take with him anything that would give away his identity in case he failed or died. But he did not know against whom these precautions were being taken. Perhaps Nogaro really believed in the existence of other races and did not want to leave anything to chance. Perhaps he did not want to indicate to possible invaders the way to Betelgeuse. Or perhaps he was afraid of adversaries that were nearer or more human. He could not figure it out. There was only the chessboard which filled one of the ample pockets of his flying suit. It was his sole clue, the only beginning he had of a possible trail.

He told himself that he was like a hunter who does not know what his prey is to be, nor even the location of his hunting ground. He looked at his watch: two minutes before eleven. On the dot of eleven he would swing into action.

The night was calm and silent. The city glowed quietly in its cold lights. The blades of a distant helicopter occasionally beat the air with a sound of rustling silk. The high towers outlined against the night sky were like vertical rays of light. Algan started the countdown. There was no point in doing it, but his lips had begun counting before he'd become conscious of it.

Five. Four. Three. Two. One.

Nothing happened. It was precisely eleven o'clock.

He waited a moment, undecided, then started to run noiselessly along the watchman's walk. He went down a flight of stairs like a cat. He had exactly thirty seconds to reach the spaceship's launching pad: every thirty seconds an electronic beam swept the entire port.

It was an invisible and undetectable beam, but if in its trajectory it alighted upon anything unusual, an alarm was set off. Normally it explored the port haphazardly. Theoretically it was impossible to avoid it because no one could tell which section of the port it would sweep. But

every thirty seconds, at least, it lit up every portion of the
port, searched all the shadows, and touched the smooth
hulls of the ships.

But on that day, between eleven and eleven-ten, at
thirty-second intervals, the sweep of the beam was not to
be left to chance. It was to follow a plan, an ostensibly
disorganized one, which would allow him sufficient time to
cross the esplanade by jumping from zone to zone without
touching off the alarm. Jerg Algan knew the program by
heart.

He counted the seconds as he sped down the interminable staircase leading from the watchtower walk. He was
three seconds ahead of schedule when he reached the
Stellar Port. He forced himself to be motionless. Three.
Two. One.

He started to run as fast as his legs would carry him,
toward a dark, distant point and he thought that from the
top of the tower he must have looked to anyone watching
like a sort of black ant dragging itself along the surface of
a plain as smooth as glass. He reached a zone of shadows
and caught his breath. This time he was ten seconds ahead
of the beam and he had to wait for it before dashing out
once more onto the esplanade.

He was a perfect target, he thought to himself as he
darted out once more. In theory, no one was to shoot him.
In theory.

The tall black prows of the ships loomed up larger and
larger. He was in a hurry to reach the shelter of their
shadows even though any comfort he derived from them
would be psychological. The shadows might have enabled
him to escape the eyes of men, but not those of the machines.

He had thought it a queer idea when Nogaro told him
of Betelgeuse's plan. Why not, he had asked, leave during
daylight, aboard a ship of Betelgeuse's fleet? Why this absurd and dangerous masquerade? Was it to deceive the
Puritans of the Ten Planets?

"No," Nogaro had replied in his chilly voice. They
would know as soon as they had heard of Algan's escape
where and why he had gone.

It was because neither Betelgeuse nor the Puritans were willing to admit, before the whole of the Galaxy, that they were worrying about hypothetical civilized races possibly living in unknown worlds beyond already explored regions. The reasons were purely political. How can we justify a refusal of a spaceship to the merchants of Ulcinor, men from Betelgeuse said, if we send an official expedition to look for the black citadels?

"If I'm caught, will I be prosecuted for piracy?" Algan had asked.

"Of course," Nogaro had replied. "But you won't be caught. Unless you want to be. If that happens, you'll be well-escorted to Betelgeuse. You might escape from there."

"It's a dangerous game," Algan had commented.

"No doubt," Nogaro had admitted. "But you are free. Do you prefer space or new lands to colonize?"

"Space," Algan had said unhesitatingly.

He was now crossing a strange forest: a metallic grove of ships; the rectilinear branches of the trees around him were antennas. Some of his hunter's instincts were aroused.

Perhaps I ought to have refused, he thought. *How can I serve Betelgeuse, which I hate?*

The answer was deep-seated. He was a hunter. He belonged to that breed which, from the beginning of time, had been used as mercenaries. He was a mercenary.

He liked to hunt—any quarry; his long outings on the depopulated Earth had had no other purpose.

There was still, among the stars, a place for men of the old world. Algan's place was analogous to a grain of sand set in a piece of machinery to be sabotaged, or like that of a ferret sent into a lair to flush out quarry.

The place of a knight on the chessboard.

Leaping from star to star.

Trying to stop a hostile king.

The black king who ruled over the Galaxy.

He began to run wildly among the tall shells of the rockets. A breath of wind sang along the shiny steel plates.

He barely heard the sound of his own footsteps, but he

thought he felt on his body the warmth of the detective beam.

Then he noticed a sound and he stopped suddenly, melting into the shadow of a huge ship. He strained to listen. He thought he heard the various clicks that fill the innards of ships: the growling of their motors, the hissing of electrons running along copper wires. The ground seemed to be vibrating underfoot.

But it was only a human step, the regular hollow beat of heels on the concrete of the esplanade.

An enemy, Jerg Algan thought, but immediately rejected the idea. A special patrol? Or, more simply still, a technician making a last-minute checkup of a ship ready to take off?

This was more dangerous than the detective beam or the maneuvering of the Ulcinor merchants. It was that unforeseeable trap that opened up suddenly underfoot during a hunt in the forest.

Algan counted the seconds. He had to start running again or the detective beam would find him in the shadows.

He slowly went around the enormous hull that was giving him temporary cover and saw, slightly to one side, the small ship that had been assigned to him. But to reach it he had to cross a zone of light, pass between two rows of ships that were as still and as threatening as sleeping monsters.

He straightened out and darted forward after his shadow which was clearly outlined on the ground ahead of him, seeming to point the way.

"Who goes there?" a voice cried.

He didn't stop, did not look behind. He merely speeded up.

"Who goes there?" the voice repeated, with less assurance this time. "Show yourself or I'll sound the alarm."

As he ran Algan tried to figure out where the voice came from. The man must have been working on one of the ships along the lighted way that Algan was following. He could not help but see him and if he had not been warned to ignore certain comings and goings that were to take place that night in the Stellar Port of Ulcinor, this was going to be the end of Algan's expedition. He would never travel amid the stars.

He thought quickly. He stepped between two ships, thus abandoning the lighted path. He knew that by doing this he might be picked up by the beam, but it was a risk he would have to run. The several seconds that it took him to go around one of the ships seemed interminable—the ship had taken on mountainous proportions. Then he slipped into the shadow of the next ship in the row and he came out again onto the lighted path.

He could hear the footsteps, which were still at some distance, speed up. The man was not afraid of coming out into the open. It was certainly a guard or a technician. The control machines knew that he must be in the port and were not concerned about his presence. And if it was a guard, he was armed and trained for a manhunt.

Algan suddenly saw him. Or, rather, his shadow. It was only a minute spot compared to the mass of ships around him, but it made his heart beat faster. He drew slowly near. He knew that he could not reach his ship without being seen.

There was only one solution. He deplored it, but he could see no alternative.

Slipping into the dark shadow of the metal ship, he struck it with his finger, making a musical sound in the silent air of the port.

"Who goes there?" the voice cried out, coming toward him.

It must have been a technician. A guard would never have made the mistake of giving away his position by calling out loud.

Algan moved quickly. He struck the hull again. The resonant vibrations ran along the sheet metal. It would have been impossible, even for a trained ear, to determine exactly where they came from.

Then he saw the man walking toward him, but unseeing, blinded by the bright light, still hesitating to sound the alarm. He stepped out of the shadows. The man made a gesture of surprise that was his undoing. He was a technician who had not been trained for fighting. He thought not of giving the alarm, but of defending himself. Algan's

fist crashed into the technician's stomach and the side of
his other hand came down hard on his neck. The technician fell soundlessly.

Algan dragged him into the shadows of the ship. The
alarm might go off in thirty seconds.

Without looking back he hurtled into the lighted alley
lined with massive, still, metal giants and crossed the
deserted, luminous plain. He ran up the gangplank of his
ship, fled down the runway, disregarding the noise he was
making, and rushed into the pilot's seat.

The ship was ready. Its generator was purring gently
and all the lights on the instrument panel were green. He
could take off at once.

Systematically, Algan began to push all the buttons. The
doors of the ship closed. Then metal safety belts came out
of the chair and wrapped themselves around Algan's body.

The ship was outfitted for fast flying and fully equipped
with safety devices.

"Good-bye," Algan murmured, glancing at the screens
that showed the Stellar Port.

He pushed the starter button. One microsecond later he
saw most of the lights in the port go on. He thought he
heard the shrieks of the sirens. Then a leaden weight fell
on him, and on the screen the lights of the port merged.

He could barely move his arms, but he managed to put
his hand in the large pocket of his spacesuit and, smiling,
gently touched the polished surface of the chessboard.

The long quest had begun, but for the time being he
could sleep. For many long weeks it would be up to the
countless controls that made up his ship to carry on.

"Have a pleasant trip," said Nogaro. Algan started. But
the voice went on and Algan realized that it was a rec-
ording.

"I can only assume everything went all right since you
got off into space without a hitch. I hope everything will
continue to do so. I want to give you some advice about
your future job.

"First of all, a warning: don't try to outwit Betelgeuse.
We could find you even in the farthest corners of the
Galaxy if we wanted to. We know you don't like the cen-

tral government. You may be sure Betelgeuse sent you on this strange mission because we're convinced that we can get from you what we want, even against your wishes.

"Don't take this as a mark of unfriendliness. On the contrary. Betelgeuse needs her rebels more than her followers.

"A piece of advice: when you reach Glania, don't try to land in the Stellar Port; you would instantly be captured. Your description and classification as a pirate have now been transmitted to all the receiving stations by Betelgeuse. We had no alternative, as otherwise our sincerity might have been questioned. Never forget you are a free agent. Betelgeuse will deny, categorically, anything you say about your connection with the central government.

"So, land somewhere on the planet, not too far from the Stellar Port, and go on foot to the city, which surrounds the port. You won't have any trouble with your rocket in crossing the detective barrages. Security, on those distant planets, is very lax, and we'll see to it that it is even more so in the month to come. Contact the man we told you about but don't tell him who sent you.

"After that, well, you're free. We'll try to show you, when you come back, that the new world that is being created is as good as the old ones.

"We trust you.

"And never forget, Jerg Algan, that I'm your friend. If the need arises, say that I sent you. My name is known here and there in space. It might help.

"See you, Algan."

See you. That postulated all sorts of improbabilities: that Algan would return from his trip to the ends of the Galaxy; that Nogaro would still be alive when Algan went back to Betelgeuse, despite the time warp, despite the frightening extension to the speed of light of the seconds spent in space.

"See you, Nogaro," Jerg Algan muttered unconsciously.

The lengthy trip in space consisted of going through a dark tunnel, of coming close to marvels without being aware of them, of defying time and death as one heard their approach in the clicking of the gears. It consisted of waiting, blind and oblivious to cold and space, of being a prisoner in the center of the whole universe, sleeping with eyes open, of drinking and of eating without appetite, reading without curiosity. The whole experience was both normal and miraculous.

All things vacillate and crumble in the space that separates the stars. Even after centuries of interstellar navigation, men still preserve the reflexes and habits of that species that has never freed itself from the Earth.

The psychological problems that arose during the course of the various phases of the conquest were solved less easily than many technical problems.

Personnel technicians responded to the challenge of the stars in two ways. At first they tried to modify man, to change his thinking, to free him from his fear, in short to have him consider as normal the oddest distortions of time and space. They tried to imprint data upon his subconscious which he could grasp intellectually. They finally succeeded in forging for him a sort of armor by subjecting him, without risk, to the most disconcerting experiments. The training was painful, but the game was worth the candle; it was the apprenticeship of the stars.

But this did not satisfy the psychologists. They knew that it was not enough for man to adjust to his conditions. They wanted to arrange things so that man would carry with him everywhere his ideal environment, in the image, at first, of the Earth, then, with the passage of time and conquest, of other worlds. So they transformed the heavy spaceships into gigantic machines that created illusions that would fulfill the need for security of the conquerors. They recreated, inside the spaceships, landscapes of the Earth, forests, fields stretching out of sight, a sun floating in the sky, starry nights. They had at their disposal the powerful magic of light. The grass in its field, the clouds in their skies, the mountains outlined against their horizons, were only illusions. But these were the illusions man needed.

However, the exploration ships which were light, quick, and maneuverable had none of these refinements—a great loss to Jerg Algan, who was on his way to Glania.

He floated through silent space in such a steady light

that he began to feel he was plunged in darkness and he also felt, while the long hours passed, as though everything that made up his individuality was dissolving inside him. His memory no longer kept track of time; it gradually became impossible for him to put a date on a past event. Sometimes all that was needed was a gesture to put him in touch once more with reality and to become himself again. But reality was so depressing that he would take refuge again in the world of sleep.

The machines looked after the ship as well as after him. G-meters with delicate gears kept the ship on course. Computers charted the safest and most economical course.

Time passed.

Days and weeks of space time; months and years of Earth time. Algan, half-asleep, dreamed of days spent on the Earth and was unable to sort out the good days from the bad. He thought of the thirty-two years of life, the dust of centuries which would cover the Earth when he returned. He thought about Betelgeuse and her infernal power and grandeur, of the Puritans of the Ten Planets and their undermining schemes; about the beginnings of various civilizations scattered about in the human Galaxy, which hoped to survive and to develop and which in turn looked forward to imposing their rule upon the whole universe despite the absurdly small number of humans scattered like sand on the face of the stars.

He thought about all the things that could happen, all the things men might accomplish; the stars they would relight, the worlds they would displace, or that they might someday create, the tremendous energies they would unleash, the beings they would meet, the other galaxies they would people, the unimaginable universes to which they would emigrate after the suns on the face of this universe had gone out one by one. He thought about everything that had been accomplished and was still to be accomplished, those planets which would never again be what they had been before the coming of man, and all the other dark diamonds of the night which were lost in the depths of their spatial solitude, awaiting the arrival of stellar ships; he thought about the men who would do these things because they had to be done, because other men had prophesied them and had wanted them done even before the nearest stars had been reached. And he told himself that they too would be torn between their memories and that strange wave, that thirst for conquest that would spur them on.

He wondered what sense all this made and decided it made very little. The only sense it did make was that man was actually doing these things; and, conversely, man made sense only because he was turning his dreams into reality.

It made sense only because it was painful. Each leap forward, each new conquest was a new birth. And every birth was painful.

Long, long ago, Algan thought, man had known periods of dormancy during which he had made no progress, when he had even lost the ground gained during the preceding eras. For a while, he would settle into comfortable immobility and allow himself to be sucked up into the quicksands of habit.

Long, long ago. For the conquest of the stars was a rebirth for the whole of humanity. And it was to be followed by an infinite number of other rebirths, perhaps even more painful ones, or other rejections of the past. One could not simply be content to be born, nor could one refuse to be born.

Man had to go on, he had to explore the huge new world that opened up before his eyes, his fingers, his virgin mind.

The history of the species was roughly repeated in the history of each individual. There was the prelogical mentality of the infant, then the apprenticeship of logical thought. Then came the adolescent's attachment to his native planet. The final stage was contact with space, with its attendant distortions of time, its pulling away from the past. In the same way the whole of humanity had been prelogical, then logical, but so closely bound by its conditions of life that emigration to other worlds had seemed almost sacrilegious. The final progression was to the stars.

Humanity was in the process of becoming stellar. It still had reflexes of fear, of distrust, like those of the adult who leaves home for the first time, and forever. It had not solved some of its inner contradictions. Was it neurotic? Perhaps the human species in its infancy had undergone such shocks upon coming into contact with reality, and was still so bruised from that contact, that the slightest deviation from the norm aroused in man's innermost being an instinctive desire for flight. Humanity had almost learned to shed its fear of space, but it still had to master its terror of time. The Puritans had solved the problem by denying its existence, by refusing to ascribe the slightest importance in their lives to time. Betelgeuse had skirted the difficulty by toting up, in the course of the years, the experiences of dead men.

Jerg Algan thought that perhaps man would grasp time as he had grasped space. He might someday send emissaries into the future with the sole aim of directing certain great projects to be carried out over several centuries. Emissaries willing to give up their country, whose sole family would be all of humanity, past and future, and whose sole country would be the universe.

And the weeks went by.

About one light-year away from Glania, the ship began to lose speed. At that distance, the sun of Glania was only a luminous dot impossible to distinguish in the fog of stars which filled that section of the sky. But its diameter increased rapidly, as Jerg Algan studied all the data about Glania that the ship contained and all the information Nogaro had left for him about the man he was to look up.

Glania was the only planet revolving around that sun. Stars having only one planet were quite rare in the Galaxy, at least in the explored regions, because most of the suns were either planet-less or had a complete system of planets. But this no longer held near the center of the Galaxy, for the probability of the destruction of a certain number of worlds increased with the stellar density.

The ship got into orbital position for the planet. The computers traced out a landing trajectory that might lead possible detectors on Glania to mistake it for a large meteor. Jerg Algan picked out, with the help of maps, a plain near the Stellar Port for his landing. Low hills would permit him to conceal his ship and it would take only a few

days to cover on foot the distance to the Stellar Port.
Then, if all went well, he could return to his ship and
plunge more deeply into space toward the center of the
Galaxy.

He saw the planet grow larger on the screens. It was a
rose-colored world, just as the Earth is essentially a green
one.

It was no doubt partly because of the vegetation, but
even more because of the relative proximity of a red star
which probably, during the greater part of the year,
lighted up the nights in Glania.

The metal straps once more came out and wrapped
themselves around Algan. For the second time he ran his
hands over the controls and got ready to feed data to the
computers. These would be analyzed and the best course
chosen.

The ship plummeted toward the surface of the planet in
order to escape, insofar as possible, the beams of detectors
sweeping the skies. It penetrated with a whistling sound
into the planet's atmosphere; its propellers went into action, braking its speed suddenly. But it had been built to
withstand shocks of that kind and complicated adapters
went into operation to soften, for Algan, the impact of de-
celeration.

The ship came to a stop a few yards from the ground.
Then it went down slowly as if held by ropes. It finally
came to rest, crushing under its bulk some of the pink
vegetation and mossy bushes that covered the plain as far
as the eye could reach.

Algan looked at the screens. The ship dominated a pink
plain that turned to violet toward the horizon. Night was
closing in; the white light of day was yielding to the red
light of night. Nothing moved. It looked as though there
were no forms of animal life on this world, as though only
a primitive vegetation subsisted there.

The reports he had read had indicated this. He got up
and opened the door. He gathered into a knapsack some
rations, first aid supplies, some tools, and slipped the
chessboard into his pocket.

Glania was quite the opposite of a deserted world, even

though it gave the impression of being a desolate planet, he thought, as he was about to go out the door. There was not a single rock, a single place that was not covered with the pink moss that seemed to be everywhere on this planet. He wondered whether, if the carpet was thick, it would seriously hamper his walking. He was thirty-five miles from the Stellar Port. On Earth it would have been a short distance, but perhaps he had been wrong to think in terms of his hunting days on the Old Planet.

He began to go down the steps, when he was startled by a dull roar. A strong wind pinned him against the side of the ship as he felt it give way. Then he understood. The ship was keeling over, disappearing into the ground.

That dull vegetation concealed a moving terrain. He paused to think. He could try to get back at the controls, start the engine, and attempt to free the ship from the bog. The maneuver would be dangerous but not impossible.

But he hesitated too long and the decision was made for him. The ship suddenly oscillated as though tossed about by a stormy sea and the wind caught Jerg Algan and flung him from the craft. He fell, painlessly, onto a heavy carpet of moss. He sank into the vegetation as if on a feather bed. He struggled, found himself on firm ground, and stood up.

The ship keeled over completely and sank between two clumps of pink, spongy, tall grasses, noiselessly, as though swallowed up by an invisible maw.

It's prow stood up, for a short time, then disappeared completely as Algan looked on, stunned and despairing. There he stood, adrift on the surface of a mud planet, unable to make up his mind whether or not to set out for the port.

He was alone, without weapons, friends, or maps, with a three weeks' supply of food, a compass, an old chessboard and vague information of the existence of a Stellar Port thirty-five miles away.

Was this what Nogaro had intended? Or had he slipped up somewhere? Had he thought the ship light enough to be borne on the surface of the planet?

It no longer mattered.

Before it had even gotten under way, Algan's mission turned out to be pointless.

Algan's progress was easier than he had anticipated. He managed to clear a way for himself between the tall clumps of moss which the red star in the sky was now tinting a blood red.

The gusts of wind died down. The succession of days and nights seemed to produce gigantic atmospheric tides every evening and morning.

He walked a number of miles, then felt exhausted. He chose a place where the ground appeared to be particularly firm. The air was soft and warm. He stretched out, tried to forget the red light on his eyelids, and fell asleep.

CHAPTER VI

Accursed Worlds

As Algan lay back with his eyes closed, on soft purplish moss, he convinced himself that the fabric of space was made up of the broken woof and warp of matter and light, facts and causes. And because he, Jerg Algan, had occupied at a given moment, a given place in space at the crucial and decisive moment of his birth, because he had grown up in a world that was known as the Earth, in a civilization that measured the universe in terms of light-years, and among men who were in the process of becoming too dissimilar to understand one another, what had happened had to happen, to him; it couldn't happen to anyone else and nothing different could have happened to him. The idea of this narrow destiny was a strange one, but it was a final conclusion; there was, in time and space, a narrow passage labeled Jerg Algan, which he would follow for the remainder of his life and, however long he lived, he would never be able to get off that track which had been inscribed in the stars.

It was a confused, upsetting thought. Never, since he could remember, had he couched it in such precise and succinct terms. He had always had, in varying degrees, a sense of freedom, but this was vanishing. He now knew that he was nothing but a pawn on a chessboard similar to the one in his pocket, but an infinitely larger one, and those who were moving him about were pawns also, even though they were probably not aware of this; and so on ad infinitum. He had often felt in the past, while hunting in the great forests of the Earth, the tight bonds between hunter and hunted that make death of the one as inevitable as that of the other. These bonds were made up of the forest, the paths, the wind, the scents, the stars, the whole universe, but they remained strangely indefinite, almost imperceptible. The quarry was vaguely and instinctively aware of them; the hunter found himself dwelling on them mentally, knowing and doubting, too ignorant about the final structure of the universe to dare venture a decision.

But now he found he was both the hunter and the quarry and that the hunting field or the chessboard was really the entire universe, in each square, a planet, or a star, or another Galaxy.

And the point of the game was simply a question.

What is man?

And there was another question, which was somehow a part of the game, of the setup which had been written in the stars from time immemorial.

Was there, in space, something other than man, sufficiently different from him not to be human?

No one had ever been able to answer this, neither bearded philosophers poring over their scribblings, nor white-coated scientists peering into their microscopes or scanning their instrument panels. No one had ever been able to answer because the time for answers had not come.

But now it had. Two huge armies, or perhaps only the populations of two anthills, had come within touching distance, but without knowledge of one another. The shock was imminent. All that was needed was the displacement of one pawn to set off the battle.

Perhaps the pawn's name was Jerg Algan.

Or perhaps he was not that important? Perhaps on the periphery of the two dark empires large numbers of pawns or guards stood ready to hail one another or slaughter one another? Perhaps his quarry and a hunter were lying in wait for him somewhere in this new world and they were as ignorant and as uneasy as he was?

He got up and shook himself. The track he had made had almost disappeared during the night. There was nothing left in the moss and pink vegetation except a sort of purple scar which would remain in the vegetal skin of the

planet for a long time to come. He wondered what was
happening to his spaceship. He supposed that it was sinking into a living abyss between heavy pulsating masses,
slipping along spongy tree trunks.

He collected his gear and set out. The night was red
and the feeble light from the distant crimson star threw a
bloody reflection on the plain. He easily cleared a passage
for himself between the clumps of vegetation. The ground
underfoot was spongy but firm enough to support his
weight.

He managed to go in an almost straight line. From time
to time he checked his compass. He calculated he was
roughly twenty miles from the small astral port. The light-
ness of his pack would enable him to reach it in ten hours
or so.

His fear had left him long ago. His nerves and muscles
had gotten back into habits picked up during his long
outings through the wild and deserted sections of the
Earth. The night was fresh, but his clothes protected him
from the cold. Every once in a while he heard a muffled
cry, a kind of long, monotonous lamentation, but he had
not yet seen any form of mobile life and the plant life had
shown no hostility toward him.

This plant life seemed to be of an extremely elementary
type, of the kind that must have been on the Earth millions of years before the appearance of an and similar to
those on Terrestrial type planets, crude models of what was
to come later.

Jerg Algan was unable to fathom the reason for the dis-
semination in space of all those laboratory cultures. Perhaps they were intended to produce some form of conscious life after a tremendously long lapse of time; or they
could be failures. Perhaps the game was being played on
such a colossally large chessboard that the less important
rules of the game escaped a mere human.

The wind came up and the mossy bushes bent and
moaned under its touch. The wind was part of the game
insofar as it hindered or helped Algan's walking, insofar as
it delayed or hurried a meeting which could be decisive
for the future of the human race.

It propelled Algan forward. It lifted him and bore him in the air, like a spider hanging on its thread, far above the red plain populated with blurred, quivering, blood-colored masses. The wind roared in Algan's ears and carried him along in the dense air just as a river carries a twig.

But the training Algan had undergone in the port of Dark preserved him from fear. He did what he should: he began to swim in the icy air. Then, suddenly, he fell.

The red plain was divided in two by a gigantic fault. Algan clearly saw the two cliffs which edged a deep valley.

He beat the air with his arms and succeeded in getting upright. His movements became coordinated and he managed to control his fall. He fell onto the ground and landed in a moss bush from which he was able to extricate himself. The edge of the chasm was a few yards from where he had fallen. The city, naturally, was on the other side.

He sat on the edge of the cliff and looked at the sky. The red star dominated the firmament, eclipsing the weaker light from the other stars which were so numerous that the entire sky seemed plastered with them. The nearness of the center of the Galaxy was perceptible, and here the stars were so close to one another that the night hardly differed from the day in quantity of light; only the quality was different.

There was nothing to do. The crevasse was an enormous obstacle, as enormous as a river for an ant. He had reached the outer edge of one of the squares and the next square was inaccessible. He had come all this way just to make that discovery.

He leaned over the edge of the precipice and saw at the very bottom the moving trunks of trees quivering in the dense air like Earth algae quivering in a sea current. Then he looked up and saw, on the opposite side of the break, the other cliff, shiny as a silver wall, gleaming under the fire of the red star. Colossal pillars, columns of cyclopean temples whose roofs had disappeared, covered with tufts of violet vegetation, stood between those high walls.

The wind had died down. And this sudden calm caught his attention. There was something in this fault that was

stronger than the wind or which controlled a current of
air able to balance the strength of the wind which had
carried him at first. He remembered that he had started to
fall just as he was flying over the edge. He felt something
warm on his face, but he could see nothing. He ran his
hand over the cold surface of the cliff and had the impression he was dipping his fingers into a liquid. Suddenly he
understood.

The banks of the crevasse were as bare of vegetation as
the edges of a river and the moss that covered the bottom
of the valley behaved like the algae of the Earth: because
it had the same texture and was subject to the same conditions. This enormous fault was a river. But, on this planet
of low density, where weight counted little and where the
air was so thick, it was nothing but a river of gas, an invisible serpentine that had dug its bed, in the course of
ages, in the crystalline crust of the planet.

It was, Algan realized, a river of gas even denser than
that of the air of the planet, a gas that probably could not
be breathed, but that might carry him, provided that he
made the necessary movements and that the current
helped. He pulled out a handful of moss on the edge of the
cliff and threw it into the invisible current; it sank slowly,
as if held by a string, drifting toward the red stillness
below.

He readjusted his gear, tightened the straps of his knapsack, and slid along the side of the cliff, clutching the crystalline brink. He felt as though he were diving into a luke-
warm liquid; then he sank and the current bore him along.
His lungs filled with a heavy, thick, viscous gas and he suf-
focated. He made a few desperate efforts and suddenly
surfaced. He breathed the air deeply. The current carried
him along without his needing to swim at all. Although his
own bodily density was greater than the gas in which he
was immersed, the surface tension kept him from sinking.
But he was as powerless as an ant carried by a river or
stuck in a drop of water.

He looked down and saw, more than a thousand yards
below, through a blood-colored fog, the open petals of
quivering algae. Then he heard a hissing sound that soon
changed into a deafening roar. Without being able to see

anything, he was dragged into a whirlwind and before he
had time to dive to escape the maelstrom he sank and lost
consciousness.

His head hit something hard and his fingers weakly
clutched a rope. He pulled himself up and filled his lungs
with air. His ears were pounding. He heard shouts and
saw, right against him, a dark bulk which hid the further
cliff from him. He was conscious of calls uttered in a human voice; he heard the sound of bare feet running along
a deck; he felt himself being hoisted and put down roughly
on a hard surface. Hands ran over him. He tried to speak
but when he opened his eyes the red star in the sky shone
brutally in his face and everything around him became
dark and silent.

It was day and with the dawn the storm that had agi-
tated the surface of the gaseous river had died down. Jerg
Algan walked from one end of the deck to the other. The
crudely built ship, hewn from the spongy and light trunk
of a pink tree was about one hundred yards long and Algan could see why. The difference in density between the
wood of the trees and the gaseous current was so slight
that a very large submerged bulk was required to carry
even a light load. The ship merely followed the current. It
had no sort of motor and more or less held its course by
means of enormous sails, submerged in the gaseous river.
The prow reared majestically above the invisible surface
and plowed through imperceptible waves while in her
stern there was an around-the-clock lookout perched in
the crow's nest.

A ship of this sort was quickly put together. Her builders had to abandon her at the end of the voyage because
it was impossible for her to make the trip back against the
current.

The sailors of this strange ship were deeply tanned
men from the center of the Galaxy. They did not pay
much attention to their involuntary passenger. They were
talking in a language unknown to him, probably an off-
shoot of one of the numerous tongues spoken in the

Galaxy out so ancient that even an experienced linguist would have been unable to make out any of it.

There were about ten of them on deck, but every once in a while Algan could hear sounds of laughing and singing from the hold and he decided this must be a team of hunters or perhaps miners who, at the close of their season, were going to the Stellar Port to peddle their meager wares.

It was difficult to tell where they came from. They could have been the remote descendants of the passengers and crew of a ship unable to leave the planet because of an unrepairable breakdown; or perhaps their ancestors had been explorers purposely abandoned by Betelgeuse in the hope that they would start another civilization. They appeared to have sunk back to an almost primitive level, but their manners were still civilized. What little they knew about their ancestors' past and of the civilization of the Galaxy made a queer mixture in their minds. They did not seem unhappy. In its own way, this planet was hospitable and these men had rediscovered the way of life of those civilizations, now almost totally forgotten, which had once swarmed over the continental surfaces of the Earth and had dispersed to the Pacific Islands.

But the new Pacific of the civilization under the rule of Betelgeuse was the whole of space: the enchanted isles or the legendary cursed lands orbited in the dark about the multiple suns of the Galaxy.

The analogy was senseless, Jerg Algan realized, as he lay stretched out in the prow of the ship on the spongy wood of the deck, turning over and over again in his hand the small chessboard with its delicate etchings and symbols of the universe, gazing at the sinuous banks of the invisible river, noting that the slow waves of the surface that lapped lightly against the high hull were like a mist.

The analogy was senseless because the scattering of the ancient civilization of the Pacific had been determined by chance and by History whereas this one was man-made. Men had been left behind on new worlds, purposely, so that History could be molded. Behind this cold-blooded concept of the conquest of the Galaxy stood Betelgeuse. Betelgeuse which, not content with having given man con-

trol of the universe, intended to have him control human
History as well: hence control the future.

A sudden cold fury filled Jerg Algan. His hands, resting
on the polished wood of the chessboard, began to shake.
All his former rancor against Betelgeuse returned tenfold.
But he could now see that his hatred had taken on new dimensions. He was only a pawn, but he belonged to the op-
position; he was on the other side of the chessboard, wherever that might be. Betelgeuse was not only his enemy, it
was also the adversary in the cosmic game.

The lookout gave a prolonged yell, and Algan, afraid of
some trick, half sat up. But all he saw was a huge net of
vegetable fibers blocking the entire width of the gaseous
river, caught here and there on the enormous rocky bolts
that stood out in the valley bed like trunks of dead trees.
Beyond that were the tall white buildings of the Stellar
Port that rose from the lavender tangle of the grassland.

The men rushed out on deck and pulled up the heavy
center board. The ship slowed down gradually. Her prow
finally got caught in the nets and stopped, almost in the
middle of the river, seemingly afloat in midair.

Ropes were connected to her sides and dragged by invisible tugs; she was pulled to shore. She came alongside
the silver cliff, just below the buildings of the Stellar Port,
and the men ran forward along the winding track made
by thousands of bare feet going between the river of gas
and the village.

The chalky white face, creased by hundreds of wrinkles,
slowly turned toward Algan. The old man sat in a shapeless
heap in a metal armchair that must have been rescued,
long ago, from the smoking remains of a ship.

His half-open eyes roamed over the muddy courtyard,
bounded at one end by a cabin of sorts made from the
spongy wood of the forests of the planet and on the other
by thorny cactus hedges imported from the Earth. These
green plants stood out strangely against the pink and
lavender vegetation of the planet.

Above the courtyard and the cabin, the Stellar Port
loomed silently, rearing its tall white bulk toward the

stars, the silhouette of a watchman. The carcasses of spaceships showed through here and there amid the invading vegetation; their dismembered keels evoked the obsolete contours of ships dating from the first period of the conquest.

The old man's thin, dry lips moved soundlessly. Then they began to let out, one by one, in weak and muffled tones, unknown words. Finally, very slowly, as though they were pushing against a heavy weight, they formed words Algan could understand.

"It's been so long, so long," the old man said.

He stopped and lifted his right hand from his knees, stretching it out to Algan. In the light of day it looked almost blue, and its skin was so parchment-like that every vein, tendon, muscle, bone in it was clearly visible.

"I have forgotten the words," the old man said. "It's so long since I've spoken this language. They're only children here, you know, children . . . you have to talk to them like children."

"I come from the Earth," said Algan in a low voice, afraid of seeing the shape crumble into dust if his voice shook the air too loudly.

"What?" the old man shouted in a sharp voice, leaning forward and seeming finally to focus his yellow, rheumy eyes on the visitor.

"I come from the Earth," Algan said, more loudly.

He took a step forward and stayed there, right in the middle of the courtyard, his feet in the mud. He undid, with a shaky hand, the straps of the bag containing his equipment, inspecting the cabin and the green, incongruous spots made by the cactus.

"The Earth is no more?" the old man said. He was obviously groping for words and Algan thought he might have expressed himself badly.

"The Earth is no more," the old man repeated. "The radio mentions only Betelgeuse nowadays."

He closed his eyes and nodded his head as though approving his own memories.

"I can remember a time," he said, "long, long ago, when Betelgeuse was just a colony and the Earth was strong and powerful and we were proud pilots. Yes indeed, proud pilots. We used to hop from one world to another in those days; we were intoxicated and never tired. We needed constant change, that's why we're still alive.

"But, you see, we were unimportant. No, not really. Those who remained on the planets we had discovered were important. They died, but before dying they had become rulers, merchants, technicians. We were only hotheads who leaped from one world to another without ever stopping to catch our breath, and we lived it up. We saw the others grow old and die; at the return of every trip, we found that the sons of our friends had taken their fathers' place and we went off again and the years piled up. But the Earth . . . there is no more Earth. I never saw the Earth again. It's finished now, as I am. I'll never see it again, you know."

His eyes blinked and he put his hands on the arms of his chair.

"Who are you, my boy?" he said. "I've never seen you around. You're a spaceman, aren't you? I thought so right away. You don't talk in that damned jargon that they use here, but I have almost forgotten the nice old language of the ships."

"I come from the Earth; my name is Algan, Jerg Algan. I was told on Ulcinor that you could give me some information."

Algan was surprised by the coldness of his own voice. He could feel, growing within himself, more and more clearly, a being whose icy lucidity frightened him. He dropped his bag on the ground and opened it. He took the chessboard out of it and placed it under the old man's eyes. He leaned down toward the wrinkled face, intently watching any change of expression.

The old man laughed bitterly; Algan shivered.

"They wouldn't believe me, oh no, they wouldn't believe me and they left me to rot in this damned world, and now they're seeking me out because they are afraid, because the Times are drawing nearer and the Masters are grumbling, because they are discovering the Accursed Worlds one by one. It was quite an expedition, wasn't it? Complete with a young skipper and brand-new ships. And this is all that remains, an old fool on his damned planet.

And not even a ship from the Earth to make an occasional stopover."

He looked up and stared hard at Algan. There still remained in his eyes an icy look that must once have been unbearable, which had gradually hardened in the light of countless suns and in the contemplation of the ghastly blackness of hopeless space.

"Who are you," he asked in his cracked voice, "that you should have in your possession the chessboard of the Masters? During the course of my long life, I've seen it just three times. Once, it was the one you have, or one exactly like it, and the other two times I saw it etched on the black walls of those damnable citadels. Who are you? Get out, leave me in peace. I've run away all my life from that memory. Or are you one of their men? Have you come to take my soul, as you did from all the other poor spacemen you buried alive?"

"I'm just looking for information," said Algan, simply. "I've come from Ulcinor where I found this board. I'm looking for some weapon to destroy Betelgeuse. I wasn't able to land in the Stellar Port of this planet because my spaceship was brought down in your sky even before I had time to land. I ended up in the underbrush and I walked for miles and miles. I was rescued by humans and I know that they won't talk or if they do that Betelgeuse will pay no attention to their gossip. I'm counting on you. You can call the men from the Stellar Port and have me arrested, but I think you'd first like to hear what I have to say."

"Perhaps," said the old man. "Perhaps." His head nodded gently on his shoulders. "I believe you. I, too, had to run away, once. I believe you. I'm going to help you. I can't do much, but I'll do it. You've gone through space; so did I. That's enough. What is it that you want?"

"I want to know exactly what happened to you from the moment the expedition you took part in disappeared, how you survived, what you said to Betelgeuse, what you told the Puritan merchants. They are the ones who told me I'd find you here and that you are the only man who can help me."

"They know everything I know," said the old man. "They already knew everything when I was still traveling

among the stars, let's see, about fifty, sixty years ago.
They know more about me than I know myself. You'll
learn nothing from me since they're the ones who sent
you. . . . But I can at least tell you the story, since you
have the chessboard."

And as he talked, Jerg Algan listened, standing in the
middle of the muddy courtyard, under a sky that was
changing gradually from lilac to pink, between two barriers of green cactuses incongruously growing on this planet.
As he listened, his fingers toyed with a chessboard of almost unbelievable antiquity, probably made by a breed in
conceivably older than mankind and immeasurably better
informed.

"We had ventured forth," the old man was saying,
"toward the center of the Galaxy. You know that the
Galaxy looks like a wheel and that the Earth is situated on
a relatively exterior part of this wheel and that, from time
immemorial, interstellar travelers have been tempted by
the idea of reaching the mathematical center of the
Galaxy, the spot where space undergoes the most extraordinary distortions and where the stars are so numerous
that the whole sky seems like a golden dome.

"We had a glorious takeoff in fifteen ships; we had a
new captain and a crew of scientists, technicians, and astronauts like me, all bursting with pride. In those days, everyone hoped to be another little Christopher Columbus
and believed in an Eldorado. But, young as we were, we
all had had some experience, and we knew that most of
the worlds that man discovers are frighteningly alien and
hostile, so we took plenty of precautions.

"We had been cruising for at least one year and we had
gone a considerable way toward the center of the Galaxy,
when we began to feel that we were entering a stellar
region quite different from all the ones we had gone
through up to then. Our instruments were no longer giving
us exact information. And our charted positions, although
we had verified them carefully, sometimes were inexact.
The physicists who were taking part in the expedition classified all these inconsistences and told us there was nothing
to worry about. They even worked out what would be the
conditions of the new space in which we were traveling so

we stopped talking about it. We were all prepared to en-
counter the most extraordinary things and these barely de-
cipherable variants in infinitely small decimals did not
bother us.

"And yet, we ought to have suspected something, for it
was the signal that we were coming into someone else's
bailiwick. At that point we were well beyond the present
human Galaxy, closer to the center of the Galaxy than
any other expedition before us had been or has been since,
to my knowledge.

"We crossed, in a layer of several light-years, a zone of
eight dead suns or planet-less ones. Not one of our astronomers was able to explain this formation, but we
thought no more about it. I now know that we had crossed
a boundary and that we had reached an area about which
the less said, the better.

"We finally discovered a star surrounded by planets. We
explored them all and on the sixth one away from the sun,
we discovered a black citadel.

"Oh, no one penetrated its secret. It was so large we
could see it from the top of the sky, as we were circling
the planet in our orbit. We zoomed down on it through
the clouds and as we landed our spaceships crushed a
large section of the jungle which covered the planet. We
had not intercepted any message and the citadel appeared
to be deserted.

"Having landed at a respectable distance, we started
toward it. It was a planet of the Earth type, with, however, a greater force of gravity, which made it more difficult for us to walk. We painfully cut a path through a
damp muggy jungle. The tremendous walls of the citadel
loomed larger and larger as we approached.

"There was complete silence. It had probably been
uninterrupted for thousands, perhaps millions of years. At
least, so we thought. Our steps faltered somewhat. We
jumped every time a twig cracked under our boots and
our hands kept feeling for the butts of our weapons.

"We could see those high walls outlined against the sky;
they were of such an enormous height that they had hidden the sky from us and threw into almost total darkness

the landscape over which they loomed. We ventured as far
as the foot of those tall, polished onyx cliffs which looked
as though they might at any moment collapse on us, for
they were planted at an angle and hung over the surrounding terrain.

"I noticed, when I was very close to the wall, that at
about three times a man's height, there was an etching as
fresh as if it had been done the day before, although its
age was probably incalculable by our means of reckoning.
It was a large-scale model of your chessboard."

"And the expedition vanished?" Algan asked. He was by
now sitting on a pink log which he had gone into the cabin
to get. He saw the walls of the Stellar Port slowly becoming luminescent as night fell and the brightness of the red
star which was beginning to tint everything blood-colored
became more definite.

"No," the old man said, "not that time. On that day, we
went back to our ships to talk over the situation. The astronauts wanted to get out as quickly as possible. They
could remember old legends and, although they didn't believe them, they were ready now to reconsider them. But
the scientists and the only historian in the group were beside themselves with joy and were worried sick at the
prospect of missing such an opportunity. In the long run,
the point of view of the astronauts, who had the captain's
ear, prevailed. We left the black octagonal citadel, higher
than the highest mountains of the Earth, but we had
marked on our maps the location of this planet with the
very clear idea that we would come back after we had
made a superficial exploration of that stellar sector.

"Barely a month later we landed on an absolutely dead
planet, a world of emptiness and silence, one of those
wandering rocks which used to terrify spacemen; it was a
purely superstitious terror in any event, since the use of
radar made it possible to avoid them and since they didn't
get in the way of space exploration any more than did the
other worlds. We had seen, from the top of our orbit, the
second of these citadels.

"You see, our minds were blown. It was the first time
that man had met any trace of another life in space, the
hope of another civilization, and this civilization was, or

had been, interstellar. There was no possible doubt. No two different breeds could have created, all the while unbeknown to the other, two such enormous and similar citadels, so visibly defying the laws governing the universe.

"We landed hastily. We built a station. We unpacked our tractors. There was no need, on this planet, to fight off the jungle and, despite the absence of any atmosphere, our work was easy.

"I myself personally went around the citadel, in a tractor. And I noticed the sixty-four squares of the chessboard, carved in stone so hard that not even our sharpest tools could knick it.

"Was it a symbol or the key to the mystery? We kept asking ourselves that question and speculated endlessly. We looked up chess in the astroship library and we found out that all of the civilizations of the Earth, scattered throughout time and space, either had known it in the past, or knew it at that time; that in some of them the game had taken on religious or magic significance and that it corresponded strangely to certain characteristics of the human mind.

"We wondered if perhaps, behind those high slanting walls, there lay the mystery of the origin of mankind and of the secret of the origin of life.

"On the twenty-fifth day of our presence in that world, after more than fifteen months of space travel, the high gates of the citadel opened. They unveiled a world of light and interlaced curves such as we had never dreamed of and which no poet on hallucinogenic drugs had ever evoked.

"Small search parties ventured forth into the depths of the citadel. They returned, staggered by the dimensions and incomprehensible layout of the corridors of that labyrinth.

"It was then that we made a captial mistake. We decided to send the entire expeditionary force to explore the citadel. The scientists had been most pressing in their request and the astronauts had stopped believing in any danger.

"I was left on the outside to guard the gates. I served as a clearing house for messages. The hours went by. I was

dozing off in my spacesuit in spite of the drugs I had
taken to stay awake, when I saw the high black gates,
which were slanted just like the walls, silently close. They
were only huge slabs, each engraved with the chessboard
signs, which pivoted inside the citadel and which sealed
hermetically the space that had remained open for several
days. My earphones registered feebler and feebler signals;
then nothing. I leaped into a tractor and made off at top
speed toward the landing pad and the rockets, but suddenly a bolt of lightning shot across the sky and the landing pad and rockets exploded, lighting up, with giant
flames, the entire horizon of the planet. I stopped the tractor, jumped off, and started to run. I had gone scarcely a
few yards when, despite the lack of atmosphere, I heard a
tremendous noise and an iron grip picked me up and
threw me on the ground, just as a smoking crater opened
up where the tractor had been."

"And that was all?" Jerg Algan asked.

"Almost all," the old man said. His voice had grown
stronger as he talked and his words, many of them ar-
chaic, were spoken more and more easily. His eyes now
shone serenely. The bitter irony which had filled them at
first had disappeared.

"Almost all," he repeated. "For five days I waited for
death because I had at most only a few weeks' supply of
oxygen and food; then men came out of the sky and rescued me.

"But they were not from the Earth, nor from Betelgeuse, nor from any known world; their spacecraft were
different from ours, their design less advanced than ours,
as a matter of fact, and they didn't understand the language I spoke any better than I understood theirs."

CHAPTER VII

On the Other Side of the Galaxy

"Men?" asked Jerg Algan.

"Men," the old man repeated, nervously twisting his bony hands. "You can believe me or not; you may think I'm crazy. The people from Betelgeuse did and they sent me into exile here; or you may listen to me silently as did those Puritan merchants from Ulcinor who never even paid up one-quarter of the sum they had promised me. But I was rescued by men. They weren't even very different from us. Their ears were small and pointed, their skins very pale, they were smaller than we are; they moved faster and more gracefully, their language was unbelievably complex, from what I could understand, and they were, by temperament, less inclined to be active than we are, but they were unmistakably men. Do you know how I learned to communicate with them? You'll never guess, not in a thousand years. You'll never work it out even though it was entirely and absolutely logical. By playing chess. That's all. You see, the king, the queen, the pawns, can be given other names and take on other shapes, but the moves are the same everywhere, and the possible combinations of the sixty-four boxes are infinite, almost as infinite as the universe itself."

"Where did they come from?" Algan asked. His heart was thumping violently and his voice had become harsh. He suddenly felt the accumulated weight of fatigue, but he struggled to keep his eyes open and to keep his wits about him.

"From the other side of the Galaxy," the old man said

quietly. His features had relaxed and his hands were now
quiet in his lap. "You probably won't believe me," he went
on. "You probably think I'm an old fool who has a fix-
ation after twenty years of exile. I can't prove anything.
But, after all, you came to get a story, didn't you? Use it
as you like."

"I believe you," Algan said softly, feeling the evening
breeze on his neck. Three pink moons were rising above
the Stellar Port; he had not noticed them the night before.
Then he noticed that they were only the reflection, on the
low-flying clouds, of the powerful projections of the tower.

It was impossible not to believe what he had heard; he
couldn't help but trust an old man looking back on his
past, who had witnessed a unique and incredible occur-
rence. But nothing was unbelievable anymore; the limits of
the possible had definitely been pushed back by ships
traveling through space at the speed of light; the world
had suddenly expanded way beyond anything human experience had encompassed, and all that space left free in
the minds of man belonged to the marvelous, to the fantastic. There had been similar periods in human history
when new lands had been glimpsed in the Occident by navigators; doubt then had also been wiped out. Then, once
the lands had been conquered, men had lost the feeling of
intoxication. But in the sky there would always be lands to
conquer and mysteries to solve.

Unless the new planets were already inhabited.

"It makes no difference to me, whether or not you believe me," the old man said in a voice that had suddenly
grown tired and quavering. "They were men, just like us,
that's all I can tell you, and they came from the other side
of the Galaxy. They were born under the same conditions
as men on the Earth, and they didn't need to tell me the
story of their species. I saw that I already knew it. You
see, it was the story of mankind, with some differences, to
be sure. Nature had been more generous to them than to
us. Their development had been appreciably lengthened,
stretched out. But it had been a steadier one. You see,
they were less aggressive than men are, and they made
fewer mistakes in the course of their history, not a whole
lot less, just enough so that they didn't have to start their

civilization all over again every few centuries. Their language was different from all those spoken by mankind, much more adaptable, but also much more complicated than man's. It seemed to me that they never had what we call a Tower of Babel. And their whole thought processes and even the makeup of their vocal systems were so different that I would be hard put to repeat a single one of their words; they never succeeded in pronouncing some of the Earthly phonemes.

"But this does not constitute a real difference. All this exists or has existed on the Earth and all men are men. And they were men also. And, like us, they wondered why they were men."

"Chance," whispered Algan. "The Galaxy is so huge."

"Maybe," the old man answered in a low voice. "Maybe. I've never quite known what chance is. But I don't believe that chance is responsible for the simultaneous development of several human races in different parts of the Galaxy nor for their coming into contact with one another at the precise moment that they learned to navigate, more or less skillfully, between the stars. And I have better reasons still for not believing it. . . . Wait a minute. I'm thirsty. Would you go into the cabin and get the metal canteen, which is on the table, and two glasses which you'll find on a shelf above the door. I can't talk very well when my throat is dry."

Algan got up and put the chessboard on the pink wood chopping block he'd been sitting on. He crossed the courtyard, conscious of the sloshing sound his boots made in the puddles which the light of the red moon had turned into an alarming shade of blood red. He had to duck as he went through the doorway and he hesitated in the pink twilit room. A thick layer of dust lay over most of the room. The removal of the chopping block had left a clean circle on the floor; two paths, one leading from the door to the rough-hewn wooden bed and one from the bed to the table, were equally clean. Algan pondered on the passage of time.

But the years that had passed here were nothing to those that had vanished in space and which provided all the old man's memories. He had been born at about the

same time as some of Algan's ancestors, so long ago that
no one on the Earth remembered their names. They probably had not left even a trace in the dusty archives of the
Old Planet or on the gravestones of the cemeteries in
Dark. He had spent a long time traveling between the
stars and the span of his life had stretched out frighteningly. He was nothing more than a kind of fossil, washed
ashore by the currents of space into this dirty and
wretched cabin. He had, along with thousands of others,
defied time and he alone had survived, but time, at last,
was catching up with him.

In its own way.

It was inscribed in the dust which covered the floor and
the furniture, which lay thickly over a piece of crystal
wrenched from some unknown mountain, over the skull of
a fabulous animal, over an ancient gun hanging on a beam
in its dried-up leather holster.

The shiny metal canteen lay on the table. Algan grabbed
it. From the shelf over the door he picked out two
glasses that the dust seemed to have spared.

"Thank you," the old man said. "I have a hard time
getting about now. Two years ago I still hunted in the forests around here, but that's all over now. Everything
comes to an end, doesn't it? Even space."

Algan cautiously sipped his drink; it was smooth and
sweet.

"They didn't come exactly from the other side of the
Galaxy, but their native land was so far away that the
stars with which they were familiar are lost to us in a
cloud of suns; charting them would be meaningless, even
to our most learned astronomers. As a matter of fact, the
expedition that rescued me was even farther from home
than ours was. I told you that their spaceships were of a
less advanced design than ours, and slower. But the passage of time didn't have the same meaning for them as for
us, at least, not exactly the same. They didn't care
whether they spent their entire lives on a spaceship or in
their own world. They thought, somewhat like the people
of Betelgeuse, in terms of continuity and of centuries. But
that's neither here nor there.

"You know that the Galaxy has been arbitrarily divided

up by our cartographers into four quarters and into three hundred and sixty sectors, like a wheel. You know that the human Galaxy is contained within the first four sectors. Well then, their home was in the twelfth sector, starting from the Earth's, at a distance from the center of the Galaxy that is at least half the distance that separates the solar system from that same center. All this merely to point out that they lived in a region incredibly far away, even for a fast spaceship.

"But they weren't all that surprised to find me. I rather thought they'd been expecting to. They had strange beliefs: one of them was that there were other human populations, in even remoter sections of the Galaxy, that around the star which is at the center of the Galaxy, there are a series of human settlements separated by tremendous spaces, that these spaces are in the process of being colonized and are gradually merging with one another, thus beginning the formation of a gigantic chain around our suns.

"These may have been nothing more than legends. I never was able to find out whether they had really found other groups of humans that had reached a level of interstellar civilization, or whether these were only nebulous prohecies which the passage of centuries had shrouded in mystery. And when I spoke with the people of Betelgeuse about that human crown surrounding the center of the Galaxy, they laughed in my face.

"But I'm positive that the men who rescued me knew something about the men of the Earth, or did know once, and then forgot in the aftermath of one of those upsets with which history abounds. They also maintained that there were no such human groupings in the regions closer to the center of the Galaxy, that those regions were, in some way, forbidden territory; they said that they belonged to the Masters who created us. But they didn't know any better than we do why those hypothetical Masters had created us. They didn't even know whether those Masters were still alive or had died. The only thing they believed was that They had planted seeds in certain regions of space for a particular, secret purpose, and that during all this time They had waited for some plan, unknown to

mankind, to go into effect and that at times, They had acted, but without mankind's being aware of it.

"You can look upon this as just a hodge-podge of legends, which is what I did for a long time. But I have come
to believe that there are, a little everywhere on the
periphery of the Galaxy, human groups that are quietly
beginning to explore their own stellar space. That's all I
can tell you.

"After a long trip, they deposited me on a planet of the
colonized Marches. I walked to a stellar port and managed to get myself repatriated in a roundabout way. One
fine day I tried to sell my information to the Puritans, but
Betelgeuse heard about it and when I had told members
of the Psychological Police Force what I have just told
you, they laughed at me and sent me into exile here. But I
know that the Time is coming."

"I see," said Algan, "but haven't you some sort of evidence?" His voice shook with weariness and irritation.

"Not a shred," said the old man. "Or rather, yes: I am
alive. What more do you want?"

"Why didn't they make themselves known? Why didn't
they go on as far as Betelgeuse, as far as the Earth, since
they had reached the borders of our empire?"

"They weren't interested. That was reason enough. They
said that things had to be allowed to happen, that contact,
then, would have been premature. I told you. They were
never in a hurry in any of their enterprises."

"Is that all?" asked Algan.

"Nearly all. Except for this: we had in common with
them (one) the fact that we were all men, hardly different
from one another, (two) the chessboard with the sixty-
four squares, (three) zotl. Their flora and fauna were different from ours, not basically, but their evolution had
been very different, almost the opposite of ours, and yet
just as logical. But they had the same zotl, which they got
from the same plant, like ours, with roots buried under
feet of rock. And like ours, it did not grow on their native
planet. We discovered zotl only after having explored
worlds other than the one on which our kind originated. It
was the same for them.

"You see, I think that in space there are three things to

be found: first the chessboard, which is probably more ancient than man; then man himself, along with life as we
know it; and last, zotl, which man in each case discovered
only at a precise stage in his development. I believe that
all three things are interrelated and that they have only
just been brought together, here and elsewhere, and that
there are correlations between them that we're only just
beginning to perceive. It's up to you to discover them."

The old man looked up and stared at the red star that
lit up the night. His dry lips were quivering and the hands
on his knees were shaking. The last breaths of wind had
died with nightfall. He got up, leaning on a cane.

"Come in now," he said to Algan. "Let's eat and rest."

Algan listened to the slow and irregular breathing of the
old man. He had rolled up in a blanket and was lying on
the wooden floor, his knapsack used as a pillow, and had
waited unsuccessfully for sleep to come.

His gaze roamed over the wooden ceiling, in the red
light of night. His nerves were on edge. The silence was
total, marked only by the light, familiar, reassuring sounds
of the night and the old man's breathing.

He could not sleep. He was thinking.

It could be that there was nothing, in all he had heard,
but unverifiable facts and legends. It seemed most likely.
Almost certainly so.

On the other hand, there was space, its extent, the
myriad worlds which dotted it, and the possibilities it held;
there were also hundreds of questions as old as man that
had never been answered. But that wasn't all. There were
other things.

There were those rumors which circulated throughout
the Galaxy, of the expectation of the discovery of another
thinking breed, human or nonhuman, that was not the result of a series of mutations of an Earth breed, like the
men of Aro whose eyes had no visible pupils.

There were many other considerations as well: Nogaro;
the curiosity and interest which the people of Betelgeuse
as well as the Puritans on Ulcinor and on the Ten Planets
showed in the tales brought back by their explorers; the
conviction shared by Nogaro and the shopkeeper of Ul-

cinor that space held certain secrets that man could not fathom.

There was the chessboard.

There were also the proximity of a silent, invisible army, the moving of pawns on a cosmic playing board, the rivalry between Betelgeuse and Ulcinor about what might spring out from space. There was Jerg Algan, with what he knew and what he did not know; his hopes, the problems he was to clear up. There were two or three expeditions that had been completely destroyed, the strange visions produced by zotl, the immense black citadels which the Puritans believed in and which the people of Betelgeuse seemed to know about.

The solution to the problem might lie in Betelgeuse. Perhaps it lay in the electronic memory banks of giant computers, in archives. It might even be that Jerg Algan was a red herring chosen to mislead the Ulcinor Puritans.

But there was the chessboard and its sixty-four squares; its general look of a double-entry table; its incomprehensible figures and its almost infinite possibilities of mathematical combinations.

Was it a symbol? The symbol of the universe?

But was it only a symbol? Jerg Algan wondered, staring at the window, feeling on his back the unevenness of the floor and on his skin the damp coolness of the night.

Or was it a reality, a key, a sort of plan; or perhaps a door that would unlock the mystery of the black citadels, placing them at the service of whoever could gather the scattered pieces of the puzzle and fit them together?

Slipping his hand under his head, he rummaged in his knapsack and took out the chessboard. With his thumb he stroked the cold, smooth surface of the wood. The chessboard was a key of greater antiquity than man and had waited patiently throughout all the human civilizations for men to learn how to use it. And perhaps the citadels scattered in space were as numerous as those grains of rice which the king in the legend promised to the inventor of the chessboard: one grain on the first box, two on the second, four on the third, continuing in a geometric progression until the sixty-fourth box would have contained more rice than the whole Earth could have produced.

Or was the chessboard a plan of space, with the trajectories followed by the pawns always representing a simple visualization of certain privileged trajectories? Or was the game of chess a roundabout way of preparing man's mind for certain tasks? And perhaps the outcome of certain games was only the result of certain problems posed by certain infinitely complex spatial coordinates.

For the problems which the chess game posed were primarily geometric, spatial, and topologic ones. These were complicated questions having to do with itineraries to be followed while avoiding the destructive effect of certain pawns placed in strategic locations.

In the middle, for example.

Was the chessboard really made of wood? he wondered as his fingers lightly touched the soft polished surface without being able to feel even the slightest space between the squares, as there certainly would have had to be if the board had been made of pieces of wood stuck together.

He had assumed from the very first that the chessboard had been carved from one or several kinds of very finely grained wood. He had thought of wood because nearly all the old chessboards he had seen on the Earth had been made of it.

He began to think that no piece of wood could have been kept in such a fine state of preservation for so long.

Unless the chessboard was a forgery, a crude trap.

He rejected that thought. The Puritans as well as the people of Betelgeuse had extremely precise scientific means for estimating the age of an object, even if forged in metal, and they would never have been fooled. And what possible reason could they have had to take advantage of him, Jerg Algan, a man from the Old Planet, a rebel against Betelgeuse, a lone wolf lost in the Marches of the human Galaxy?

And then there was zotl. Zotl and the chessboard.

Zotl, that strange drug which was in no way harmful, which affected the nervous system and enabled it to perceive certain otherwise incomprehensible realities.

Psychologists said they were illusory, dangerous, traumatizing. But, countered mathematicians and physicists, the universes which could be explored by drinking zotl

were perfectly logical, much more so than a man's dream;
they were as logical as the universe itself.

Cenesthetic delirium the psychologists retorted. Just a
crossing of nerve fibers. You see what you ought to hear
and hear what you ought to see.

Neurologists took no interest.

The chessboard and zotl.

Zotl was a door that half-opened on incomprehensible
worlds. And the chessboard was like a pass, a plan which
allowed you to take your bearings and to glimpse certain
worlds that were comprehensible and quite real.

Zotl and the chessboard.

They complemented each other, like a lock and a key,
so long as there was a man's hand to slip one into the
other, and to push open the door.

But the man had to do more than just take a quick look
into the room that had been unlocked; he had to enter it
boldly.

Boldly.

There were the chessboard and Jerg Algan.

He got up suddenly in the pale light which bathed the
room, and shook the old man.

"Wake up," he shouted, leaning over the wrinkled gray
face.

"What is it?" mumbled the old man, sitting up and blinking his eyes.

"Get up. I'll explain. I need your help."

Algan watched him slip into a worn and patched as-
tronaut's uniform.

"The sun isn't even up," quavered the dry, trembling
lips.

"It doesn't matter. I can't wait any longer."

"So?"

"I've been thinking about what you were saying. I need
some zotl to try an experiment. Have you any?"

"No. What use would it be to me?"

"Do you know anyone on this planet who has some?"

"Zotl roots don't grow here. And the people are poor.
They can't afford that luxury. No, I don't know of any."

The old man opened the door and they went out. The
courtyard was just as muddy and dismal as it had been the

night before, but the ending of the night cast an enchant-
ment over it. The surrounding jungle looked as though it
were being devoured by flames; the house itself seemed to
be consumed by an imaginary, cold brazier. But the high
buildings of the Stellar Port rose like blocks of ice, even in
the heart of the deep red night.

"Hold on," said the old man. "Maybe the port commandant. You'd have to go see him. Perhaps there is a cargo
of zotl in the cellars of the Stellar Port. Maybe he drinks
it. I doubt it, because he comes from one of the Puritan
worlds. But I don't quite see how you're going to talk him
into letting you have a little zotl even if he has some.
What can you give him in exchange? Anyway, tell him I
sent you."

"All right," said Algan. "I'm on my way."

"It isn't even daylight yet. Wait a bit."

"There are no days or nights in stellar ports," Algan
said, "and I've already waited too long. I want the captain
to remember my visit. Good-bye."

"Good luck," the old man said, but his voice betrayed
doubt and distrust. He watched Jerg Algan close his knapsack and move off along the steep path which led to the
high bronze gates of the Stellar Port, between the
wretched hovels which made up the only street of the little
town. He shrugged and went back to his cabin.

"You can't go in. Not at this hour of the night. And besides, you're an alien."

There was a steely air about him in his uniform of supple metal. His unmoving fingers rested on the buttons of
an instrument panel; he could unleash all the fires of hell
around the gate. His eyes shone like polished silex. His
helmet gleamed like the nugget of a fabulous metal. He
was, in his unruffled obstinacy, immortal and invulnerable.
He was the representative of Betelgeuse and he knew that
the whole might of Betelgeuse was at his command.

"I am a free citizen of the Galaxy," Algan said loudly.
"I have the right, night and day, to enter stellar ports."

"In theory, yes," the guard said in his icy voice. "But
here, at night, even the leaders sleep. You ought to do the
same. You can speak to the captain tomorrow."

"I act only under his authority," Algan said. "You haven't the right, on your own, to forbid me entry into the port."

"I see you know the rules," the watchman said with the shadow of a smile. "Very well; if you can prove that you're a free citizen of the Galaxy I'll let you in."

"I am a human," said Algan. "That ought to be enough."

The guard shook his head.

"You're a foreigner. Where did you come from? You're not native to these parts." His voice dragged condescendingly over the word native. "And you've never come to the Stellar Port. There aren't that many visitors to this forsaken hole; I'd have noticed you."

"That's immaterial," Algan said. "How do you know that a patrol ship from Betelgeuse didn't leave me on some sector of this planet that your detective beams don't cover. Didn't your screens register the approach of a ship?"

The guard's expression changed slightly.

"Maybe," he said. "Maybe. But even if that were so, I've had my orders. I could be punished for not obeying them."

"I don't think that your commandant will do so if you let me in. If you don't, I guarantee nothing."

The watchman closely looked over Jerg Algan once more. The rumpled and dirty clothes, the unshaven face, the fatigue in the stranger's eyes were not reassuring.

"Nogaro sent me," Algan said abruptly.

"Nogaro? Where did you hear that name?" The guard's voice had become commanding.

"He sent me. That's all."

"Nogaro," the guard said thoughtfully. "I thought he'd died. OK. I believe you. But I'm going to call the commandant and he'll decide himself whether he'll see you now or wait until morning. I wash my hands of the whole affair."

He pushed a button and the high bronze gates, on which were inscribed in enormous letters the name of the planet, Glania, opened and admitted the stranger who stepped in alone, onto the enormous deserted esplanade of the port and went off toward the luminescent tower.

The commandant's back was resolutely turned to Algan as he looked at the sky through the great bay window at the other end of his office. The light of the rising sun darted along the thickets which bordered the eastern horizon and the black aerials of the port stood outlined against the sky that was still a dark red; they were like the overly symmetrical branches of calcined trees.

The commandant was small and brown but, with age, had become regrettably portly and his disposition had soured. He wore a wide leather belt and gazed longingly at the Stellar Port, empty of spaceships, and at the sky, empty of any messenger from Betelgeuse.

The hours sometimes dragged on Glania.

"You have a proposition to make?" he said unpleasantly. "Let's hear it. I'm listening."

"You don't even know who I am," Algan observed.

"That's immaterial."

"Let's rather say we'll discuss that later."

"I'm waiting," the commandant said.

His hands, which he had been holding behind his back, began to move. The first clear rays of the sun overflowed from the horizon and the light and the color of the sky began to change. Every night and every morning, the contest between the red light of night and the white star of day was renewed. The white sun was a huge spider which spun, on the whole surface of the sky, a web of rays which almost instantly spread over the entire horizon and the faraway deep red star which seemed to grow pale and to flee was invariably caught.

And every night it was the other way around. Legends were beginning to take form in Glania, about this continual struggle between night and day.

"I've come to offer you the means of attracting Betelgeuse's attention to yourself," Algan said slowly. "Maybe even to get a couple of promotions, or to have you transferred to a world closer to the center."

"Well?" replied the commandant. He began to laugh,

but it was a hollow sound. He stopped abruptly, turned around, and looked Algan up and down.

"What the human Galaxy needs most at the moment," said Algan, "is a means of interstellar transportation that is almost instantaneous. The gadgets we use to increase the speed of our spacecraft are no longer adequate. I believe that the central government of Betelgeuse would show its gratitude to the man who could invent a new procedure."

"You, for instance?" said the commandant icily.

" 'Who' is immaterial. Let's say that I am now in the experimental stages. Let's say that I need a product I cannot obtain here. Let's say that you have some. Would you be prepared to let me have a small quantity so that I can go on with my research? I would be extremely grateful to you, as would all of the Galaxy."

"What do you need?" the commandant asked, staring into the distance, beyond Algan, beyond the walls of the room, beyond even the planet, into a world of dreams to which only the commandant held the key.

"Some zotl," Algan said softly.

The commandant's eyes at once lost their faraway look and focused on Algan. He placed his hands on the desk and leaned over toward Algan. Then the blood rushed to his face and he started to laugh so hard that tears rolled down his cheeks.

"Zotl, my boy," he said when he had quieted down. "Is that all? Are you quite sure that's all? But, first, what makes you think I have any? Are you crazy? Asking me, with a cock and bull story, for zotl. Zotl to travel among the stars. Let me tell you that lots of people have tried to get drugs from me; some even tried to steal, but this is a new one. You really believe your story, don't you? You're paranoid, just paranoid."

"Zotl is not technically considered a drug," Algan replied coldly.

The commandant stopped laughing.

"I've had enough of you," he said. "Now get out."

"Zotl is not a drug," repeated Algan, "and if you have some, I'm prepared to pay you for it. It's a perfectly legal transaction. Only the Puritan worlds look upon it as a narcotic, even though they have never been able to prove any harmful effects. But here we're in a world completely controlled by Betelgeuse. You're allowed to sell me zotl if you have any, and I think you do. And Betegleuse will show you her appreciation some day."

The commandant's eyes resumed their faraway look.

"I do have some zotl," he said. "I take it, sometimes. The days drag by in this forsaken land. It's not illegal. You know that, if you're a secret agent from Betelgeuse. I ought to have suspected something of the sort."

"I'm not a secret agent from Betelgeuse," Algan said. "I'd rather tell you before you discover it for yourself. I've never even set foot on Betelgeuse. But I need zotl and I'm ready to pay ten times its price. Let's put our cards on the table, shall we?"

"OK," said the commandant. "Have you any money?"

"No."

The commandant became visibly irritated.

"You're crazy."

He reached for a switch concealed in the moldings of the desk.

"Don't do that. I said I didn't have any money on me, but not that I couldn't dispose of a considerable sum. As a matter of fact, I represent a considerable sum. I need about twelve zotl roots. Set your price."

The commandant thought for a moment. It was a huge sum.

"About five hundred unities."

"I'll offer you five thousand. My name is Jerg Algan. And there's a price on my head. Five thousand unities, in fact. An even exchange. You can check in your latest bulletin."

They looked at one another for a while without speaking. Then the commandant broke the silence.

"I suppose you're under the impression that you've covered every contingency. But what would you do now if I detained you without giving you the zotl?"

"That's easy. The money put on my head will be paid only to the man who has taken me prisoner. The offer does not hold if I give myself up to a representative of Betelgeuse. So there can be two versions of my capture.

Either you caught me after a rugged chase and you get the reward. Or I state that I gave myself up and you get nothing."

"They won't believe you," said the commandant, biting his lips. "They'll believe me sooner than you."

"Sure," said Algan. "But they'll believe the evidence of a lie detector even more. Then I'll be forced to tell the truth. They'll believe me only when I say that I gave myself up. And you'll be prosecuted for perjury. On the other hand, if you accept my conditions, I'll never have to go through a lie detector test. The law allows a criminal to refuse the detector even if he is heavily incriminated. I have nothing to lose."

"How do I know you won't double-cross me as soon as you've been arrested?"

"You can't know. My word is as good as yours, that's all. I've been open and aboveboard with you in the hopes that you'd understand that my word is good. And, after all, there would be no point in my double-crossing you. It's Betelgeuse that's paying, not me. You run some risk, but it's worth it, believe me."

"Five thousand unities," the commandant said quietly. "It's almost the price of a secondary planet. Damn you if you really are a secret agent from Betelgeuse."

"There's a price on my head," Jerg Algan reminded him. "You can check."

"All right."

The information about him flashed on the screen. Ships' positions, signals, warnings, then the rhythm slowed down and the film stopped abruptly on a picture. Jerg Algan's.

The portrait was startlingly lifelike. It must have been taken on the Earth, in the port of Dark, while Algan was undergoing training. Yet it no longer completely corresponded to reality. It was an image of the past. Algan's face was now harder, browner; his eyes were deeper, more brilliant.

Instructions followed. A detailed description, the charges leveled against him, a picture of the ship in which he had fled, and the amount of the reward offered to any citizen of the Galaxy—be it a civilian, a soldier, or an officer—for his capture. And, in red letters: *To be captured alive. Under no circumstances to be shot. Probably not dangerous.*

"They really seem to want you," the commandant merely said.

"Much more than you think. They need me as much as I need zotl. And for the same reason."

"OK. Follow me."

And as he walked behind the commandant, Algan reflected on the information given in the bulletin. The men from Betelgeuse had not mentioned the charges they had leveled against him nor the threats they had made. They alluded only to the theft of a ship, and in mild terms. But that had not been the real crime, if crime there had been, since they themselves had given Algan the opportunity to take over a ship. The truth was that they wanted to be sure that Algan would be returned to them as soon as he had discovered something and before the Puritans could grab him.

They had loosed Algan into space much as a ferret is loosed into a burrow, cages being placed at all the openings in the hopes of catching him after he had flushed out the quarry.

But there was one opening they had overlooked.

"There's obviously no point in trying any monkey business," said the commandant. "As you probably know, no weapon will work in any part of the Stellar Port, unless I give the order, locally, to do away with the inhibiting field. Furthermore, my guards would swing into action at the faintest out-of-the-way sound. Let me add that never, in the long history of the human Galaxy, has a gang of criminals, even in large numbers and armed to the teeth, succeeded in capturing the Stellar Port."

"No point in harping on that," said Algan. "I didn't come here to fight."

They went through a door which shut silently after them. A section of wall pivoted, revealing a deep recess which contained a deluxe zotl press and a sizable pile of roots. Algan whistled.

"I owe this setup to my predecessor," said the commandant. "He was recalled to Betelgeuse, one fine day, because of some obscure matter of trafficking. I found this

long after he had gone, quite by accident. Legally, it's
mine."

The tone of his voice showed he was on the defensive
and that he was still not sure that Jerg Algan was not a
secret agent from Betelgeuse.

"Put a root in the press," Algan said.

He took the chessboard out of his bag and put it on a
low table. He placed an armchair facing the table, sat
down, and lay both his hands on the chessboard, each finger in a square. Then he took his hands off and examined
the fine engraving, the figures etched by a diamond stylus
aeons ago. They appeared—or was it an illusion?—to be
trembling. He tried to think of something besides what he
was going to do. He had no idea what was going to happen to him. But it didn't matter. Given his situation, this
was the only solution. If it was a solution. He watched the
zotl root being crushed by the heavy piston, and that reminded him of the Earth, Dark, and the shopkeeper of
Ulcinor.

Only a few days had gone by since his departure from
the Stellar Port of Dark, at least, a few days for him; he
had traveled from one end of the Galaxy to the other at
almost the speed of light along very short routes, but on
the Earth, perhaps whole decades had passed.

And his friends were dead.

He stared at the half-full glass the commandant had put
before him and pushed it aside.

"Squeeze another root," he said. "Double the dose."

"You're risking insanity," said the commandant.

"No," said Algan, "that's a myth. I know what I'm
doing."

"I hope so," said the commandant.

He was eyeing the chessboard suspiciously.

"What's that?"

"I'll tell you later," Algan replied wearily.

The second root vanished under the piston.

He had no way of knowing what the optimum quantity
of zotl was. He had to experiment. Nine chances out of
ten he would fail.

Unless, behind his back, without his knowledge, someone was pulling the strings of the puppet he knew he was.

He emptied the glass and placed his fingers on the chessboard, haphazardly.

Or was someone guiding his fingers?

He saw the commandant staring at him, unbelieving; he saw his eyes widen. He saw the commandant's lips move to form a cry.

Shapes and colors quivered and became fuzzy.

"Good-bye," he said in a last gasp.

Then he disappeared.

And the chessboard with him.

CHAPTER VIII

Beyond Dead Suns

It was a gray, unstable universe, fuzzy, imprecise, made up of changing curves and constantly changing orbits. Then, gradually, certain lines became clearer. Straight lines. And gray clouds emerged from definite areas either lighter or darker. Lines separated the areas. It was a chessboard.

Algan tried unsuccessfully to move. He wasn't supported by anything. In the first moments he had been conscious of falling, then that feeling had vanished gradually as the contours of the immense chessboard on which he was became clearer.

He was a pawn on the chessboard and he was traveling along certain complex trajectories, skipping from square to square. His skull hurt agonizingly. He didn't know why he was jumping from square to square, but he told himself that there must be some reason, that he knew the reason, but that he couldn't remember it: it was deeply engraved in his subconscious.

He had a headache, as if he had been making a concentrated mental effort. He had instinctively made some calculations based on certain data, but he didn't know how he had done this. He had used the result of his calculations, but he did not know why he had to skip from one square to another on the chessboard.

Or perhaps his calculations, his migraine, and his unplanned moves on the sixty-four squares were all related. Algan remembered number sixty-four as a relatively low number. How could the chessboard be so enormous if it was made up of only sixty-four squares? He was struggling in a cotton-like fog; memory had fled; there was nothing around him that he could understand.

"What's my name?" he asked aloud. But the sound of his voice never reached his ears. One problem filled his mind. Which square should he move into now? He thought hard. Then suddenly, his mind cleared; portions of his brain which had been inactive until then stirred. He had the feeling he had won a victory, but he did not know over what.

The solution came to him. He started moving again on the chessboard.

"What's my name?" he wondered again.

It was a rhetorical question. He had not the faintest idea what a name was. All he knew was that he was faced with a number of problems that took the form of ideal moves to be made in a game of chess.

There was no meaning in a name. Only the solving of ideal itinerary problems had any meaning.

Sixty-four squares were not much, but the number represented a colossal quantity of possible itineraries, obstacles to be avoided or overcome. This required a no less colossal amount of calculation.

The human mind functions, partly, like a calculating machine, he thought. *It solves the problems put by . . .*

By whom?

By no one.

By me, Jerg Algan.

He had solved the problem and he knew who he was. Jerg Algan. Thirty-two years old, a rebel against Betelgeuse. A human. A refugee who had just escaped from Glania by means of the chessboard. He was on a mission.

He had a frightful headache.

I drank too much zotl, he thought. *I must have had the D.T.'s.*

The gray shapeless fog which surrounded him parted. He suddenly started to float in the heart of a black universe interspersed with lights. Space.

He had solved the problem of the chessboard. He had left Glania and traveled through space. He had extracted the root of the equation: man-plus-chessboard-plus-zotl.

And he had not lost his sanity. He had come into contact
with reality once more. Could he be sure? He was floating
in the heart of a black space sparsely sprinkled with stars.
The fear of falling gripped him. But the reflexes which
had been inculcated in him during his training period on
Earth allowed him to regain his self-control.

He was not really falling. When his eyes had adjusted,
he saw that he was resting in a huge, black, hard, cold
armchair in front of a table made of the same kind of material, on which the chessboard lay. His fingers were resting on squares. The air was cold and serene, alive; there
was a whiff of countless ages. He looked up and saw stars
shining in a black sky; they were few, reddish, extinguished and reflecting the light of other stars, or in the
process of dying; but much farther in space luminous
regions shone, distant agglomerations of suns that were
difficult to tell apart.

He sniffed the air and decided that it was perfectly safe
to breathe. As he considered the blackness of the sky, it
seemed to him that he was suspended in emptiness on a
planet that had no atmosphere, that there was nothing between his eyes and the dying braziers burning in space.

But, he thought, it was possible that an invisible dome,
perhaps a purely energic, unsubstantial one, in the depths
of the ocean of space contained an air bubble capable of
sustaining life. It was possible that his visit had been pre-
ordained and that enormous citadel in space had been
built solely with his future presence in view.

It was an odd idea. It seemed inconceivable that a fabu-
lously ancient breed, which more than likely was nonhuman, could have built, a little everywhere in space,
gigantic stopping places for the sole purpose of helping
the human species to conquer the stars. Unless this breed
had itself been a human one and that the machinery it had
built in ancient times was of such a degree of perfection
that it was still in operating order.

He got up from his chair and walked around the enormous circular room. It was lit by a gray light which did
not prevent the rays shed by the stars from being visible.

The walls of the room were bare and black. And in one
precise spot, exactly opposite the armchair and the table

on which lay the chessboard, Algan discovered, etched in the wall, a chessboard in each of whose squares were incredibly delicate etchings.

These intrigued Algan. They were the same ones he had seen on his own chessboard, but they followed a different sequence. He crossed the room, picked up the chessboard, then compared the two.

There was no difference. His memory could have failed him, but he doubted it. The figures on his chessboard had moved. This could mean that the chessboard was a reflection of the universe and that each change of position of the images represented the solution of a problem. It could also mean that there existed a relationship between the universe, or between the Galaxy anyway, and the chessboard, and that any change in the chessboard corresponded to a displacement in space.

Was it an almost instantaneous displacement, or did it spread out over a period of time? He could not tell. All he knew was that as far as he was concerned an extremely short period of time had elapsed during the trip. He felt his face with his hand and noted that his beard had not grown much. But had the Earth grown older? That was the question. Had thousands of years passed over Betelgeuse while he was traveling over that distance; or was it only ten seconds? If he ever returned to the human Galaxy, would he be dealing with Nogaro, or with his distant descendants who would not even know his name?

There was no exit from this room. Yet the chessboard engraved on the wall could be a lock. He put his fingers at random over the squares, for he had no precise question in mind. His fingers had barely touched the middle squares when he became aware of a light, crystal-like sound and a small section of the wall directly under the chessboard pivoted.

He hastily stepped aside, unsure about what might pop out. All he saw, in the opening, on a black pedestal, was a gray globe.

He went up to it and saw that the globe was a sort of vessel filled with an amber-colored liquid—the liquid extracted from a zotl root.

So, the black citadels really were the key to the prob-

lem of man, chessboard, and zotl. Zotl plunged man into a
trance which made it possible for him to *glimpse* other
universes, other worlds, along new directions, and the
chessboard made it possible for man to *move* in space
toward those worlds.

To move directly, without having to make use of all the
costly and slow paraphernalia of space transport, and stellar ports scattered on hard-won planets.

Perhaps the black citadels were the infinitely more advanced equivalent of stellar ports. And just as Betelgeuse
was the spider in the web encompassing the stellar ports
throughout the human Galaxy, there must be in the heart
of the Galaxy an alien and ancient intelligence lying in
wait, which made decisions and moves, all the while
watching over the men who dared to venture out in its
labyrinth.

But he did not know into which part of the Galaxy he
had been transported by the effect of the zotl on the chessboard. Judging from the scarcity of stars and the blackness of the sky, it might be that the huge and dead world
in which he was at present was situated on the edges of
the Galaxy. The suns which he could see appeared to be
dying. But he remembered what he had been told, on
Glania, by the old pilot, about that string of dead suns
which a lost team of explorers had met on the way to the
center of the Galaxy.

An incredible amount of energy had probably made an
obscure furrow in space, long, long ago, perhaps even before the appearance of life on the Earth, and had accelerated in incredible proportions the process which controls
the aging and dying of stars. Therefore the center of the
Galaxy was surrounded by a desolate barrier of midget
white stars and purple suns which marked the boundaries
of forbidden territories. He was far less removed from the
center of the Galaxy than he had feared. But this proximity itself made no sense if he thought about it in terms
which he was accustomed to using. It took light more than
fifty thousand years to travel the distance which separated
the center of the Galaxy from the outer edge of the huge
constellation of suns. Astronauts in their spaceships, moving about in the stratosphere, could have done so in a

fraction of the time that they actually took. But that was still too long. He realized for the first time how silly words used in the human Galaxy were.

Men had conquered only one province in space, one suburb of the Galaxy; only a few thousand planets had been explored—yet there were millions of stars that surrounded them. He shivered. His earthbound assurance, his human self-sufficiency suddenly evaporated. He was unable to remember the glory and power of man. All he could now see on the screen of his mind was the incredible, multitudinous swarm of sparks that made up a cluster of stars. He was overwhelmed by the size and complexity of the problem. He closed his eyes. But it suddenly occurred to him that he had something just as complex as the Galaxy itself, his mind, and its neurons, which could make innumerable associations. The universe posed almost unlimited problems, but humans had at their disposal an instrument capable, consciously or unconsciously, of solving them. They had been given an instrument and the means to use it. He had to know how and why.

He took the globe in both hands and drank the zotl. The liquid cooled his throat. He crossed the room, sat in the armchair, placed his fingers on the chessboard, then scanned the sky. The stars became blurred and changeable.

The transition this time was much easier than the first time. He did not have a feeling of being torn apart and the migraine which had been oppressing him vanished. He floated for a while in grayness while cerebral centers of which he was unconscious coordinated the movements of his fingers on the chessboard and the displacement of his body in space.

He was moving at random. His goal was to find some indication of the nature and provenance of the makers of the chessboard and of the black citadels. He was hoping that by jumping from world to world he would at last reach the end of an immeasurable trip: the place from which had come the builders, or the Masters, as the old pilot on Glania had called them.

But there were millions of suns and planets in the Galaxy and there might be almost as many black citadels. Perhaps this was a hopeless journey.

The citadels were all alike, he soon noticed, and the
room in which he found himself at the end of each trip
was always round and topped by an invisible cupola, but
the starlight that filtered through the cupola and the colors
of the sky were always different.

Once he thought he was at the bottom of the sea because the color above was so low and green. He could not
see the light of any star, only the steely gray light of an
enormous sun. The planet was so large that he could make
out the line of the horizon through the cupola, above the
black walls of the room. He looked fixedly at low blue
hills whose immobility was worrisome; there was no
movement anywhere. It was an inchoate world on which
life had not yet begun, perhaps because it could not support life. It was an alien world, enclosed within its walls of
clouds.

He left it for a shining rock that was moving through
star-hung skies. He thought he must be approaching the
center of the Galaxy because the stars were so numerous
there. They appeared to touch, to crush one another. The
sky was golden and the sparse dark places looked like
black stars that had irradiated from the night. Another
time he saw ruins stretching out under a dark red sky afire
from the proximity of a giant red star. Those ruined palaces had not withstood time the way the black citadels had.
They must have been the work of a lesser breed, comparable to humans, who had hoped to compete with the
power of the Masters. Or perhaps these beings had committed suicide in a fit of bloody madness. It was a drama
that Algan was unable to reconstruct. In any event, odd-
ly-hewn stones in geometric shapes, stretched up toward
a flaming sky forming a circle around the citadel.

He began to move about with greater and greater ease
within the restricted area of the chessboard. He did not
yet know how much control his mind had over the sixty-
four squares and the curious designs with which they were
decorated, nor which portion of his brain was being used,
but he did not much care. He was now able to move all
over the Galaxy. He even found that he could land on a
planet at a place other than the top of the black citadel,

that he could regulate his flight in the stratosphere and get back into normal space or land in the middle of a star, or on the surface of a deserted world and then, in a split second, take off for one of the black citadels. Whenever he traveled there was a kind of protective screen between himself and danger from the outside. He felt that he was simultaneously in normal space and outside of it.

While he traveled, he never felt hungry, thirsty, or tired. He was situated outside of time. He felt fulfilled as he never had before. He was at last performing the task for which he had been created. He was the master of the stars and space, more powerful than the men of Betelgeuse or the Puritans of Ulcinor and the Ten Planets. He was doing what none of them had even dared dream of.

Worlds of ice and worlds of flame, diamond planets and sand planets, marshes and deserts, clouds heavy with storms, luminous fogs, crystals aligned in infinite rows along plains of purple mud, stormy sterile seas—these were what he saw from the unchanging domes of the black citadels. He began to wonder whether the citadels were not giant spacecraft—or a single spaceship—which he was trailing along with him in his journey over the chessboard of the universe.

The worlds he visited were nameless, inhuman ones, which could never be colonized, but they had a beauty that was more pure, more austere, more vibrant, than any he had read about in the books about the conquest of space. On these light was refracted, surfaces distorted by the pull of tremendous gravity. But the conditions prevalent inside the black citadels were always the same.

His eyes had their fill of giant stars floating in the sky like balloons of fire that were larger even than Ras Algheti or the Auriga Epsilon which had been the admiration of the astronomers of the heroic age. Once when he had completed an incredibly long journey, at the end of a cascade of suns and planets and had reached the central regions of the Galaxy, he discovered new wonders, a space whose multiple curve was visible, an unbearable blaze of colors, stars orbiting around one another, bumping into one another like balls. Space itself, filled with gas and

dust, seemed luminous. He saw ringed stars; he saw, shining in the distance, globular cumuli each of which represented more stars than man had conquered and which
were only a drop in the bucket of the Galaxy.

His regard and admiration for the builders of the black
citadels increased even more when he realized that he was
traveling not only in space, but in time. The light of the
stars in the center of the Galaxy, which he had seen on
the Earth, had been traveling for thousands of years, yet
he now saw those suns as they had been just a few years
before. The builders had erected a civilization in propor-
tion to the universe, as immeasurably vast in relation to
human accomplishments as the whole of the stellar parts
was in relation to an anthill.

And they were dead, he told himself.

For a long time he was unable to find any trace of
them. The empty rooms did not contain the slightest clue;
it was as though they had been only waiting-rooms, abandoned long ago, or as though they had been built for a
purpose that had never materialized.

But all that changed as he came closer and closer, by
means of an irregular spiral, to the center of the Galaxy.
A presence, a vague scent floated in the air, suggesting a
recent passage, a trace, nothing that was as yet visible. Algan noticed that increasingly the black citadels were located in gigantic worlds that were surrounded, to judge
from the color of the sky, by an atmosphere consisting of
hydrogen.

Once, a long vibration shook the tiled floor of the room.
Algan waited, but nothing more happened. Hours passed
in silence and he felt fatigue slowly and dully engulf him.
He left without having heard the vibration again. He was
not worried about being lost. The very idea of getting
back to Earth seemed unnatural.

But there were more and more signs that indicated the
end of the journey. He had thought that he'd been placing
his fingers at random on the chessboard, but actually—he
realized—he was solving problems mysteriously put to
him.

Then suddenly he found himself in a room of a different
kind. Its black walls had wide doors set in them. He

rushed out and saw a golden sky and lavender-colored fields that were not unlike those of the Earth; there were low hills outlined against the horizon. He felt on his skin the warmth of thousands of suns. Fatigue overwhelmed him and he dropped onto the purple grass. It felt soft and cool.

He knew he had reached the world he'd been looking for, that he had reached the end of his journey. He raised his head a fraction of a second before hearing the voice.

"Greetings, robot," said the deep, musical voice, in Algan's language.

"I'm not a robot," protested Algan. "I'm a man."

"In our language," asserted the voice, "man is a synonym for robot."

CHAPTER IX

Betelgeuse

The room was huge and bare. An ashen light oozed from its solid walls. Eight men were seated around a glass table, talking and drinking. Their clothes seemed to be woven of silver; on their fingers rings shone with gems. Whenever they stopped talking silence reigned, a heavy, deep silence unbroken by any sound or vibration.

The room was located three hundred yards below the surface of a world near Betelgeuse. Two hundred and fifty yards of solid rock and fifty yards of steel separated it from the floor of the Government Palace. These were the eight men who held the fate of the human Galaxy in their hands.

"You're still a young man, Stello," said a brown man with deep-set black eyes. "We know all about that kind of uprising. We don't believe in using force. Time is on our side."

"All right," said Stello, who was sitting to the right of the man who had just spoken. "But we've had three cases of mutiny in less than a week. That ship off Olgane whose crew, led by their captain, is openly engaged in the most objectionable sort of traffic; that station on Oldeb V which refuses to admit our agent and, last of all, that expedition on the outer Marches which is refusing to leave the world we had sent them to explore. Don't you think our fleet will soon abandon us either to devote themselves to looting or to settle on that paradise that is said to exist somewhere in the Galaxy? Some positive action must be taken about the fleet."

The seven men dressed in silver turned toward Stello. There was an odd gleam of amusement in their eyes. They all appeared to be in the prime of life and yet time had left imperceptible marks on their foreheads and on their slender white hands.

"I shall vote no," said the man with the black eyes. "Not because the use of force frightens me. But because destruction is futile and brutal. No, believe me, Stello, any fears I may have about the future of the human Galaxy come from something else. You are inexperienced. We have known other periods. We have seen entire stellar systems secede. And time has always brought them back to the fold. There are ways of dealing with this other than sending a war fleet. And how do you know that it wouldn't be a good thing to have the crew of a ship settle on a distant planet? Their descendants will come to us for help and protection."

"Perhaps," said Stello, putting down his glass on the crystal table. His eyes scanned the faces of the others, lingered on their cold eyes, their thin lips, and their high, intelligent foreheads.

"We have unlimited means at our disposal," said Albrand, whose hair had been tinted silver by time. "And yet, Stello, we are curiously unarmed. We maintain order in the Galaxy, we are the most powerful tyrants human history has ever known, but space and time protect with an almost invincible barrier those we want to strike down. I don't know what label will be given to our period in history. Perhaps it will be looked upon as a strangely perverse epoch, or a singularly free one. I hope we'll be judged only by our intentions. We want man to rule the Galaxy."

"We're well aware of this," said Olryge in his icy voice. His red hair and his eyes that sparkled like rubies were a familiar sight on many a ship of the Betelgeuse fleet. "And we also know that you are quite content to rule this empire of the Galaxy, even if you are not entitled, as were the kings, emperors, or dictators of the past, to glory and to the hurrahs. I've known you for almost three centuries and we have talked a great deal about your mission. Are you growing old?"

"Be quiet," whispered Albrand, his fingers trembling

with rage, but his features impassive. "I am not so ambitious as you. I'm quite satisfied to be an administrator. All I want is the welfare of mankind. I don't care about the honors."

"You'd sell us all down the river to bag the title of all-powerful master of this Galaxy."

"You're judging me by yourself, Olryge."

"Stop it," said the dark-eyed man. "Can't you see that the worst danger lies within ourselves, within this group? Have you learned nothing during your long lives? Whether it be ideals or ambitions that rule you, can't you keep them under control? Can't you understand that, faced with the immensity of the space that we have to conquer, we are all equal? We ourselves, the Machines which fill the Government Palace over our heads, and those of our people who are traveling here and there in space are the secret rulers of the Galaxy. It is our impetus which has enabled mankind to forge ahead so fast. And yet you'd destroy all that with your quarrels. Come, Albrand, I can remember when you never spoke of anything but peace and you, Olryge, remember your dreams about the power and the freedom you wanted man to have."

"We're far from it now," said Stello. "Sometimes I wonder whether we've accomplished anything at all, whether the secret power we wield makes any sense, whether the anarchy that prevailed at the beginning of the conquest was not better than this iron rule which logic forces us to maintain."

"You've certainly done a complete about-face, Stello. A few moments ago all you could talk about were punitive expeditions, repressive measures, and now you're full of doubts," said the black-eyed man.

"I don't know. I'm always afraid our empire will crumble. Shall I outlast it? But I know that wouldn't make any sense. My existence depends entirely upon it; I live only for it. I am less master of my fate than the lowliest of the spacemen I met when, years ago, I made the rounds of our conquered territories. The very thought robs me of my sleep. I think about all the stars we have conquered and about the sparse population on them and about the ease with which those bonds could be severed and about the whole human structure that could just drift off. At times, I say to myself that it is just one huge body of which we are the head, our agents are the eyes; the body is gradually dying and we, the Immortals, remain. I think we could not survive the destruction of that body. And fear breeds violence, doesn't it, Olryge?"

"You've been reading too many early philosophers," grumbled Albrand; the others remained silent, plunged in thought.

"There's something in what Stello says," interjected Fuln, as he put his thin, slender hands on the cold table. "We are the masters, yet we would be powerless without those few million Immortals who travel all over the human Galaxy, and without those electronic brains that process the data we give them and which are even more indestructible than we are. Sometimes I wonder whether we are not all of us the slaves of those Machines, whether they have always waged their own wars without regard to us."

"You're living in a dream world!" shouted Albrand. "The Machines put forth suggestions; we make the decisions. Billions of humans believe that their existence depends upon decisions made by Machines. But think back to the first Immortals who began this work, long before you were born; they decided to hide behind Machines and to rule secretly because they knew that men would be more willing to obey orders given by a mechanized ruler than those given by men, even immortal men. The Machines of Betelgeuse have become the symbol of the continuity of the human Galaxy, but we are in fact that continuity."

"Perhaps," said Fuln. "Perhaps. But on what do we base our decisions? On the basis of data provided by the Machines. Let's suppose those data are carefully selected. Let's suppose those Machines are themselves controlled by someone? One of us?"

"It's an old, old problem," the dark-eyed man said gently. "I've never been to a meeting where the question did not come up. And no solution was ever found. The problem for the Immortals is that experience has made them suspicious and yet they want to be sure about everything. But that's impossible."

"Never mind who makes the decisions," Stello threw in. "We are moving toward a goal. That's the problem."

No one said anything.

"We'll never reach it," Olryge said gloomily.

They looked at one another and waited.

"Do we really want to reach it?" asked the dark-eyed man. "When the central government was set up near Betelgeuse and the Immortals took it over, the precise goal, which was kept secret, was to turn the human species into a breed of Immortals able to take on the entire universe and to conquer, in time, or in spite of time, the farthest reaches of space. Has that goal been altered?"

"No," they answered in chorus.

"But is this what we really want? Do we still want it? Do we still want the whole of the human race to be like us? I'm not sure. I think something has happened that the founders of the central government did not foresee. Mankind was developed in space like a gigantic organism, as Stello was saying just now, whose every planet is a cell and whose head is Betelgeuse. And we are glad, in some ways, to provide that organism with goals and directives. We do not want it to dissolve, not even to produce a higher form of organization. We do not want it to die because we'd die with it. We are trying to keep it alive, such as it is, as long as possible."

"All right," said Olryge. "But do I need to remind you why our goal was not immediately realized? The end result required that certain secondary goals be reached first. Immortality bestowed upon the entire species would have imperiled the future of mankind. Our predecessors were afraid of overpopulation, famine, war, and I don't know what else. The human Galaxy wasn't large enough at the time and mankind not sufficiently mature. Are they now?"

"We can't be sure," the black-eyed man said with a smile. "We'll never be sure. We only know that we have conquered or explored a huge number of habitable planets, that there are still others; that mankind is only a tenuous veil stretched among the stars and that our conquest

will not last unless we can soon call upon large numbers
of people."

"Is mankind mature?" Olryge repeated.

"We could discuss it to the end of time, and we still
wouldn't know," the dark-eyed man said. "It was decided,
once, that the Immortals were immortal and the rest of
humanity was not. I'm not sure this arrangement would be
feasible nowadays, yet we continue to use the same criteria whenever the question of recruiting new Immortals
arises. It was also decided that immortality would remain
a secret, the best kept secret. But can we keep it forever?
Wouldn't it be better to let it out before someone else
does?"

"What do you mean?" Stello asked.

"We have kept our immortality secret only at the cost
of Draconian measures and because the time warp, result-
ing from trips made at the speed of light, has shrouded
our existence in mystery. But can we keep it up? I doubt
it. Just imagine what would happen if another group of
Immortals were to show up in the midst of the human
Galaxy and wanted to challenge our power."

"Humanity, as we know it, would die," said Fuln.

Their faces, normally so impassive, became anxious.

"We've overcome all crises of this sort," said Olryge.

"So far," the black-eyed man went on. "But how much
longer can we keep it up?"

"What do you suggest?" Albrand asked.

"Immortality for the whole of the species."

No one spoke. Stello drained his glass. Olryge's fingers
began to twitch nervously.

"I vote no," said Olryge. "There is no danger yet."

"Are you sure?" countered the black-eyed man.

"Before I believe in it I'll have to see the danger with
my own eyes. The Galaxy is secure. All our data confirm
this."

"The Machines process our data. Have you already forgotten what Fuln was saying just now?"

"Figments of the imagination."

"Are you really sure?"

"We have no enemies we know of."

"We have masses of them, Olryge. Where have you

been? Have you forgotten, among others, the Puritans
from the Ten Planets?"

Olryge laughed.

"Ghosts. We brought them completely to heel over fifty
years ago. They learned on which side force and history
were."

"Perhaps fifty years is long enough to forget. Don't ar-
gue, Olryge. You're wrong to think always like an Immortal. Don't forget that ten years is a long time in the life of
a man and fifty years stretches over several generations.
I'm not sure that we, Immortals, could stand defeat as
well as simple humans do. You'll notice that whenever a
wave of humanity is crushed, another rises to take its
place; we, on the other hand, never forget the lessons we
have learned. Our defeats are final. Men's are as transitory
as their lives. Ulcinor has never forgotten its old dream of
hegemony. They have recently tightened their regulations
pertaining to aliens. They have of late been in something
of a turmoil. Sometimes they remember things we have
forgotten. They hope, whereas we calculate. It doesn't
take much more to topple an empire."

"Their power is nothing compared to ours."

"All right, but that wasn't true yesterday, or, rather,
fifty years ago. It could grow again."

"We'll stop them again."

"Perhaps this time we'll lose."

"Nonsense."

"I expected that from you, Olryge. We must realize that
we are neither omniscient nor omnipotent, and that we
could be beaten. And I should prefer that that defeat not
extend to the whole of the human Galaxy. I should like to
have Immortality bestowed upon all mankind. Oh, I don't
expect to win you over, Olryge. You remember what
Stello said a little while ago, about his fear of seeing the
humans whom we rule, die. You feel the same. We all
share the same fear. But if we must go, let us do so by
choice.

"Let's let mankind rule the entire Galaxy," pleaded
Stello. "We have years and years, if not whole centuries,
still before us, before we reach the outer limits of that is-
land of space."

"We'll reach them, if the time is granted us," said the black-eyed man. "We probably would have to make men immortal in order to accomplish this, because there aren't enough of them. But let's leave that aspect of the problem aside for now. I just don't believe that we will have the time. We have enemies inside the human Galaxy. We may have some outside it."

"I don't understand," Stello, Fuln, and Albrand said in chorus. The others merely opened their eyes wider.

"Let's assume that, in spite of all our efforts, the Puritans were to discover the secret of immortality. That would be disastrous, wouldn't it? All our plans would become obsolete. And, weak though the Ten Planets are, they could successfully stand up against us within a hundred years. Especially if they threatened to give away our secrets. Up to now, the Puritans have made use of only the best known substitute for immortality—travel through space. They sent out some spacemen to cruise at the speed of light during a few months or a few years, and when they came back from their journeys, decades or sometimes centuries had passed; in this way contact with the past and the future was constantly maintained. The men of the past could force their descendants to carry out plans made centuries earlier. But those men just led the lives of men. They died too soon. And now they are aiming at something else, at a more positive form of immortality. Toward a continuity between the past and the future which looks very much like ours."

"Where would they get it from? Their laboratories have been destroyed. Their scientists led along false scents."

"Have you never wondered, Stello, why this secret of immortality remained a secret so long? There was a time when no secret of this sort could have been kept, no matter how closely guarded. That time was not so long ago, but do you know what lies between that time and ours? Space, nothing else. We've been able to keep the secret because there is, between worlds, an immense barrier of space. And nothing can travel through space without our explicit consent. That is why it is difficult to reach or leave Betelgeuse. There have been, from time to time, vague rumors, but there are so many legends careening about in space that they were soon forgotten.

"But space, which is our ally, can also become our enemy. It isolates us, but it also isolates other worlds and other secrets. And it could be that the Puritans received the promise of outside help and that that is the source of their hope."

"Help from outside the human Galaxy?" said Fuln.

"Just that. Does the name Jerg Algan mean anything to you?"

"Almost nothing," said Stello. "But I think he is an important factor in the Puritan mythology."

"They called upon him when they were fighting fifty years ago," said Albrand. "But I seem to remember he died about two hundred years ago."

"I'd like to be sure," said the dark-eyed man. "The Puritans are all stirred up because they say Algan has come back."

"They're looking for something to back up their legends," Olryge said.

"Perhaps," said the black-eyed man. "But Jerg Algan was seen a few days ago on Betelgeuse."

"You pay too much attention to legends. You're just a dreamer, Nogaro," said Olryge.

Nogaro's dark eyes scanned the gray walls of the subterranean chamber. The shiny tiles were inscribed, in tiny characters that time would never erase, with the names of all the Immortals. Hardly a thousandth of the surface of the walls was covered with inscriptions. The whole of the past history of the human Galaxy was summed up in those names and on those walls. But there was a fair chance that there would be no future history for the Immortals.

"Try to convince me, Olryge," said Nogaro.

Betelgeuse. Jerg Algan came out of the frozen darkness of space, blinked, and recognized his surroundings. He stood opposite a huge glass wall covered with mathematical symbols, behind which the eyes of giant computers opened and closed. He was in the very heart of the Governor's Palace; above his head there floated a large red sphere, symbol of Betelgeuse ruling the human Galaxy.

The room was empty. The first time he had visited it, it had been full of people and he had come in through the great door, along with travelers from a thousand different worlds, in order to admire the Machine upon which their lives depended. But this was his second trip to Betelgeuse, and the Masters had sent him to the very heart of the problem.

Night must have fallen on the only inhabited planet in the system, the one on which were the Government Palace and the Machine. It was impossible to tell from the light because for centuries neither light nor heat had varied in the great hall of the palace. But this room was empty only at night after the great bronze gates had been closed. They were stronger and larger replicas of the gates that enclosed, from one end of the human Galaxy to the other, the white fortified walls of the Stellar Ports.

Detectors might already have picked up Jerg Algan's presence in the great hall; the Machine might already have made a plan of defense. But Algan was unconcerned. He looked down at his feet and examined the floor tiles. It was strange that during all the centuries that had passed since the Government Palace had been built, no one had taken any interest in the particular design of the black and white flagstones.

It was a chessboard. Sixty-four gigantic squares.

In each of the squares there were designs, that were almost imperceptible, which looked like the fine scratches that time, chance, and the feet of travelers might have made on the vitreous tiles.

Algan did not bother to make them out. He had already studied them during his preceding trip. He had other things to worry about! Hatred and triumph were jostling one another in his mind. And something else.

Loyalty.

During his first trip to Betelgeuse he had come to a deserted place at the end of one of the parks that circle the city. He had come out of the night, his eyes still reflecting the cyclopean splendors of the center of the Galaxy, and he had seen, spread before him, the largest of the human cities. And whatever his faith in the genius of the Masters, he realized that the city stood up well in compar-

ison with the black citadels and the wonders, buried in the
depths of the stars, which he had seen. Betelgeuse represented the greatest success of human madness and genius. Government ships had brought here all that was best
in the human Galaxy.

Algan relaxed. Two centuries of practice had taught
him to go through space effortlessly. He filled his lungs
with fresh air. He sniffed the smell of grass and damp
earth. He got up and slid noiselessly between the trees,
toward the city.

He looked like a human. And yet he was not entirely
human. The Masters, who, long, long ago, had created
men, had changed him, improved him somewhat. His
heartbeat was slower than that of men, consequently he
was less prone to fatigue. He could vary his metabolism,
and survive a long time under difficult conditions, or cause
any wounds to heal quickly. He was impervious to germs
and viruses. And even death had passed him by. He was
immortal.

He saw the domes and the spires of the city between
the trees, as the pink vapor of the morning rose under the
heat of the red sun. Spaceships went across the sky from
time to time or rose from the neighboring Stellar Port.
Their design had scarcely changed. Their performance
may have been better. But this was not what surprised Algan. The real surprise lay in Betelgeuse and in everything
that Betelgeuse contained.

He had traveled bodily, in time. Two centuries had
elapsed since he had left the human Galaxy. Two centuries
on the Earth and almost two centuries for Betelgeuse, if
one took into account slight variations in time. But all
sorts of people had been traveling in space since there
were spaceships able to travel at the speed of light.

However, few people ever reached Betelgeuse. Betelgeuse, which, on a human scale, seemed to be situated
outside of time.

Algan was going slowly along the walks of the deserted
park. He didn't care whether anyone noticed him. It was
unlikely that he'd be recognized. So, at least, the Masters
had decreed. He was wearing the same clothes he had
worn when he left Glania. But there was little likelihood

of his being noticed, for one saw the most extraordinary outfits on Betelgeuse.

He noticed strange plants in the park. They were green. Green plants. He hadn't seen a tree for almost two hundred years. He remembered that the founders of the central government of Betelgeuse were born on the Earth, a long time ago, and that they were still homesick for their native planet.

He tried to remember Dark, and the plains and oceans of the Earth, his friends, the jungle, the jumble of dirty streets, the fights, the warmth of a butt in the palm of his hand, the sweat of a hot day, and the icy breath of a winter night.

All that was over and done with.

It's unbelievable that all this once existed, he thought. *Dreams.*

The sand crunched underfoot. This nerve-racking noise had not changed; it was a sound that reminded him of waiting, of long walks along the seashore, and of hunting in the deserts of the Earth. The sand had not changed in two hundred years. It was always the same, on whatever planet. Sand was what remained after palaces and mountains had collapsed. But he, Jerg Algan, had changed.

Dark and the Earth, Ulcinor and the Puritans, had been submerged in the bituminous fog that the sound of wet squeaking sand underfoot evoked. He had once wanted to see humans again, to walk through the maze of streets in Dark, or to browse in the small shops of Ulcinor among tall, masked figures.

He had done it. He had leaped from one point to another in the Galaxy; they had never been real journeys, like the one he was undertaking now in Betelgeuse; those had been visits, strange experiences which could have been exciting.

But which hadn't been.

Dark was nothing but a rathole at the end of space, and Ulcinor a bear's den. Worlds and cities had altered in two centuries, but not to the point where he couldn't recognize them. The change was in himself.

He was now, and he knew it, a spaceman. His cities were the stars that shone in the sky. He felt a vague pity

for men burrowing into their houses at the bottom of the
oceans of cottony atmosphere that surrounded the habitable planets. He had heard, during his brief stay on Ulcinor, that his name had taken on a somewhat symbolic
meaning for shopkeepers of the Ten Planets, but he did
not trouble to find out whether he'd been recognized. The
problems of humans no longer interested him. He was a
spaceman and proud of it. He was not one of those astronauts who cross the great voids in a steel hull, blind,
terrified, and paralyzed by the thought of the many dangers lurking. He was a true spaceman, able to follow the
paths of outer space, to leap from one square to another
on the chessboard of the stars, to solve the finicky problems of trajectories and to checkmate the opponent's
King: Betelgeuse.

He was—and he had recognized it proudly—a pawn on
the chessboard of the stars. A pawn of the black king who
ruled over the Galaxy. He found it hard to remember the
period when he had been on the other side. It was so long
ago, so confused, so unreal.

He had at that time been a human.

Now, he was a Robot.

The light from the cupolas and spires of the city shone
softly through the branches of the trees. But the massive
outline of the central Government Palace dwarfed them
all. Algan reached the outer limits of the park without
having met a single human being. Suddenly he was in the
city; his footsteps rang with a new sound on the road and
he was in contact with humans once more. He saw them
hurrying along; in their faces joy, sadness, disgust, fear,
old age. They filled him with pity.

He thought of the cities that were going to perish, of
the spaceships which would be stopped in orbit, of deserted roads, of faces which were going to become expressionless, and of the bodies that would become immortal. It
might take years before all this took place, but years no
longer meant anything. The age of cities, spacecraft, and
humans was over. And now he knew that it was what he
had always wanted, what all humans had always wanted,
that that destructive fury they had manifested in every
period of their history was only the confused anticipation

of the time to come when neither life, nor cities, nor ships,
nor stellar ports, nor the heavy, costly, crushing organization of human powers, nor time, nor death would have
meaning anymore. It was soothing, strange, to think of all
those beings still bubbling over with life, as if they were
superannuated and dead, reduced to dust; and yet he was
forced to because that was what was going to happen.

It had already happened at other times, in other places,
in other portions of the Galaxy and in other galaxies. The
age of provinces in space and the age of man had ended.
They had thought themselves masters, albeit always conscious of their shortcomings, their inadequacy; they had
proclaimed themselves the final product of the universe,
but they were only the means to an end, robots.

He must not, he thought, let his face be too void of expression, or his walk be too unconcerned. He might attract
attention.

He mingled with the crowd and followed the wide ave-
nues to the Government Palace. There were magnificent
apartment buildings along the way. He recognized how
splendid they were, but only, he said to himself, as a pale-
ontologist recognizes the strength of vanished species and
the perfect articulation of their limbs, none of which,
however, prevented them from dying.

The gigantic square in front of the Government Palace
was in itself almost as great a wonder as the stars, as the
countless worlds in space, or the constructions of the Masters. Moving roads furrowed the vast metal expanse like
rivers of silver. There were colossal statues, on crystal
pedestals, of human figures molded in the same indestructible bronze as had been used to make the gates of the
Stellar Port. Their calm gaze looked confidently into
space, seeming to watch over the continual activity of
spaceships plowing the skies. They were as high as mountains and their hands, raised toward the immense sphere
of the dazzling star, looked big enough to shelter a
spaceship. Farther along the way there were strange pieces
of sculpture—abstract ones, knot-works of curves and
light which represented man's idea of the universe,
complicated, mathematical, elusive, and hostile struc-

tures, splendid in their colored multiplicity. On the way to
the palace of Betelgeuse, Algan, carried along by the
gentle motion of the moving roads, saw etched in glass
and metal, complex symbols that depicted man's conquest
of the universe. The processes regulating the birth, life,
and death of stars, those which controlled the dance of
electrons or the perpetual overlapping of waves were inscribed there. Here, man's admiration was equal to his understanding and art sprang naturally from knowledge.

But it was, Algan told himself, a last twig on a dead or
dying tree. It was time for man to discover what he really
was.

Going through the gigantic gate he closed his eyes
unconsciously as he faced the enormous sphere of red fire
representing Betelgeuse, which floated above the crystal
cupola. It was shining high overhead, but its brightness
was such that for an instant he thought that it was plunging toward him. He pulled himself together and saw, below this midget sun, a bright ring of white lights which he
recognized as a replica of the Galaxy.

He smiled. Men had thought for so long that they
would rule the Galaxy that they had become accustomed
to the idea of a future victory and thought they had
achieved it.

The moving sidewalks stopped at the entrance to the
great hall. Algan went forward onto the huge black and
white tiles, each big enough to hold a fairly large
spaceship and he saw before him the crystal wall which
separated visitors from the Machine.

Everything in the great hall had been contrived to impress visitors. The palace had been built centuries before,
when the central government had been located on the
third planet of the ones that rotate around Betelgeuse.
From the very start of that remote time, it had been sin-
gled out to store the archives of the human Galaxy and
the Machines which process the endless data.

Countless visitors had gone through the great hall which
was a meeting place for the world of the conquered stars
and the mysterious and abstract one of the Machine;
where the past and the future crossed. All kinds of people
came: barbarians from remote lands, scholars from an-

cient worlds, astronauts plowing the frontiers of space, sol-
diers from Betelgeuse who wanted to take a look at the
sanctuary for whose defense they were responsible, ar-
chitects filled with awe by the pure, immense lines of the
crystal vault, merchants wanting to see the Machine which
assured order in the empire; men of all breeds and colors,
size and intelligence, wearing the most exotic or the most
ordinary clothes. There were footsteps that echoed with
assurance on the tiles, and others that shuffled along the
cold floor; people drank in with their eyes the high metal
pillars, jostled one another like a swarm of ants, put questions to the Machine and listened with unflagging interest
to the answers it gave.

For the miracle of the Machine was that it knew everyone and everything and that it answered every question. It
was a miracle, repeated daily, one of secondary importance which the less complicated portions of the Machine
were programmed to deal with, but it served as legendary
and tangible evidence that the Machine governed with
unerring fairness.

Historians claimed that since the very beginning of time
there had been Machines to help men make decisions, by
defining for them the nature of alternatives of the problems to be solved. The Betelgeuse Machine was merely the
logical result of the invention by man of a long series of
devices to aid the memory. But, the historians continued,
this one had been devised to replace man rather than to
help him, in order to insure that the government of the
human Galaxy would have a continuity which human
frailty would not have made possible; men seemed to accept its decisions more willingly than they would have accepted orders from other men.

A small section of the Machine could be seen behind
the crystal wall which divided the great hall in two.

Some of the tourists thought that the mass of giant
tubes, memory banks, revolving cylinders, sparks, screens,
and copper wires were all that the Machine consisted of.
Others, either less naïve or more knowledgeable, suspected that there was more to the Machine than met the eye,
that it occupied more space than there was room for in
the great hall of the palace, that its data were piled up in

dark underground vaults and that its decisions were worked out far from human eyes.

Data came pouring in from the entire Galaxy; it did not matter how recently for the Machine was the past, the present, and the future.

Some wondered whether the Machine was not merely a screen, a part of the decor behind which a tremendous power was concealed, but they generally did not dare to ask that sort of question out loud. Least of all would they have asked the Machine.

Algan shouldered his way through the crowd hurrying along the black and white squares. When he was near the crystal partition, he saw the cells through which the Machine could be questioned. They were famous throughout the human Galaxy. Children on remote balls of mud dreamed of some day coming here, questioning the Machine and getting an answer. But many grew up, aged, and died without ever realizing their dream. It was probably because so few of the billions of inhabitants of the planets had come to Betelgeuse and seen the Machine that the Government Palace kept its magic aura.

The cells had been dug out in the crystal partition. They were alveoli with mirror-like facets. There were hundreds of such cells all in a row at the foot on the glass partition.

Algan went into one. Facing his image, he looked deeply into his own eyes. The Machine's motto was: "You must seek the answer in your innermost self."

All the sounds of the world were stilled. He was alone with his image at the bottom of a luminous space; he saw a long, thin face, bony features, and bright, cold eyes. He had never before seen himself quite like this. Nor had he ever heard his heart beat, nor felt his breath like this. He moistened his lips and started to speak; but then waited uncertainly for the Machine to ask him a question. Suddenly he understood that there was no Machine, that it did not exist, that there was nothing except his reflection and that only his reflection would answer.

He could almost see what a human's reaction would be.

"Well, what do you want to know?" asked the Machine.

The voice was flat, without overtones.

Algan thought. He decided to ask a routine question,

one which millions of men, dead or alive, had uttered, convinced, deep down, that they were profaning an oracle.

"What obstacle must I overcome?" he asked.

"Loneliness," the Machine answered unhesitatingly.

Was it the usual answer to that question, or had it given Algan the answer suited to his case?

Loneliness. He had not thought of it for a long time, nearly two centuries.

"My name is Jerg Algan," he said. "Do you know me?"

There was a pause.

"Yes," said the Machine evenly. "You were born on the Earth. You ought not to be here now."

"No, of course. Can you tell me where I've come from?"

He knew that that question was going to cause confusion and fear in Betelgeuse. He waited a moment.

"No. I don't know. Wait a minute. I'm going to check up."

"Don't bother. Just try to find out where I'm going."

He smiled at his reflection and suddenly disappeared.

For the second time he was in front of the Machine. But it seemed to be asleep. The crystal partition was almost completely dark. Only a few tubes were blinking. The mathematical symbols etched in the surface of the glass shimmered gently.

Hatred and triumph jostled inside him, for the last battle was near. He started to walk unhurriedly toward one of the alveoli of the Machine.

CHAPTER X

Through the Crystal Wall

"Two hundred years," said Stello.

"Yes, two hundred years," Nogaro repeated.

His face hardened. He put his hands on the table and stared at the seven men.

"He must be immortal," said Stello.

"I think so," said Nogaro.

Silence. Suddenly they were afraid. Afraid of a stranger over two hundred years old who had appeared with no warning from space, alone, empty-handed.

"Didn't he take a long trip on a spaceship?" Albrand asked. "A few years spent at near the speed of light could perhaps . . ."

"No," said Nogaro. "The Machine is positive about this. He disappeared about two hundred years ago in the region of Glania, a small planet on the border of the central regions."

"He was never seen again?"

"Never. Fifty years ago, some of the people from Ulcinor who had been imprisoned at the time of the Puritan repression claimed they had seen him. But this was never confirmed."

"Could the Puritans have put him in a state of hibernation in order to use him as a weapon at the right moment?" Olryge asked.

Nogaro shook his head.

"How did he get to Betelgeuse?" asked Voltan, one of the oldest of the eight, older even than Nogaro. "Does the Machine know?"

"No," said Nogaro. "All it knows is that he did not come on a spaceship. At least, not on one of ours. Human spaceships, I mean."

They were all silent again. They felt something in the air stretch and vibrate. Everything they had accomplished in centuries past was evaporating, dissolving, disappearing in the frightening uncertainties of the future. For the first time they were afraid of what was going to happen.

"Outside help," grumbled Olryge, his eyes flashing. "You were speaking of it just now."

"It's the only logical solution," Nogaro replied coldly. "I am the only one of us who knows Jerg Algan. He was already a strange man two hundred years ago. I wonder if now, after all that time, he's even human."

He made a face, not that he was afraid, he was just simply consumed with curiosity. He knew why Algan had left, he knew that he had been successful. What had he found in the center of the Galaxy?

"Tell us what you know, Nogaro," said Stello.

Nogaro turned and stared at him. *Shall I tell them?* he wondered. *Shall I tell them that I acted on my own initiative, two hundred years ago, thereby possibly endangering the whole of the human Galaxy? Shall I tell them that I'm sure I was right because there are problems more important than the well-being of the Galaxy? Or shall I say nothing and let them flit from one theory to another? Does the Machine know?*

But whether he decided to speak or be silent, he thought, nothing in the future history of the Galaxy would be changed. Someone had to do what he had done. As to what Jerg Algan had discovered and what had become of him, that was another story.

"Do you think he has transmitted his secret of immortality to the Puritans?" Stello asked.

"I don't know," Nogaro said. Lines of fatigue were suddenly etched on his face. It had been a good life, all these years, asking questions, making decisions, learning. It had been good, then weariness had set in, a heavy, gray weariness. It would still have been good, he thought, if the world could have remained quietly, peacefully, the same.

A kind of terror began to grow inside him. *Am I that*

old? he wondered. *Have we condemned men to immobility, the Galaxy to stagnation?*

"I don't know," he repeated. "Do you imagine this is of the slightest importance now? I spoke about the Puritans a little while ago only to get your attention. But can't you see that their agitation doesn't mean anything anymore? Can't you see that the problem is no longer ours, that our ships are useless? Can't you understand? Another race, another civilization, which is immortal, is at our gates, able to travel in space without our knowing it. . . .

"Perhaps that will be good for us. Do you see now why I am asking immortality for the whole of the race?

"I stick to my vote," said Olryge. "Our power is tremendous, intact; we have not yet been attacked. We're still in control here."

"I wasn't thinking of war, Olryge," said Nogaro. "There are other forms of competition."

"Who was this Jerg Algan?" Voltan asked in his deep voice.

"Two hundred years ago, or perhaps a bit less," said Nogaro, "when I was not yet a member of the Council, when I wasn't even on Betelgeuse, I met Jerg Algan. I was only an Envoy, one of the millions of Immortals who are the watchdogs of Betelgeuse on the remotest worlds, who listen and transmit, who are the eyes, ears, and hands of Betelgeuse. Shortly after our meeting, he disappeared. I had made friends with him. He was about thirty years old, had spent all of his youth on the Earth. He had just been picked up in the port of Dark and recruited under the usual circumstances. The first time I saw him was on the ship that was taking us to Ulcinor. I was favorably impressed by him. He was energetic and persistent, intelligent and sad. I think I'd have liked him to be one of us. He hated Betelgeuse for he was, you see, a man of the old planets for whom the past was more important than the future and who called a spade a spade. The name of Betelgeuse for him was synonymous with tyranny.

"At that time I was looking for someone to carry out a plan I had made. I looked over Algan's credentials and found them satisfactory. The same problems existed then as today, only circumstances were different. We kept looking for traces of another civilization. There was some evidence that pointed to an interesting zone in the general direction of the center of the Galaxy. I was carried away by the idea of sending an expedition there, and I still am. But the Puritans on Ulcinor were watching us closely because they were afraid we'd find the means of wiping them out financially. They had information that I lacked. I arranged things so that it would look as though Jerg Algan was being sent by both sides, which is probably why the merchants of Ulcinor and the Ten Planets boasted about his support.

"We had already sent several expeditions to the center of the Galaxy, but they had all failed. A couple of them even disappeared altogether. Extraordinary tales began to make the rounds of the Galaxy. I thought it was high time they were stopped.

"But I was only an envoy and I hadn't the power to put Jerg Algan in charge of an entire expedition. To do this, I'd have had to get the Council and the Machine to agree and that would have taken too long. I decided to have Algan steal a spaceship. I knew that the Stellar Port authorities would do what I told them to and so, when we landed on Ulcinor, I made the necessary arrangements.

"One night, Jerg Algan slipped out of his sleeping quarters, knocked out a technician, stole a rocket, and left. I knew that he headed first for Glania, where he hoped to find the beginning of a trail that I had indicated. And there he vanished. He was on the border of the central regions of the Galaxy, and suddenly he disappeared."

"Under what circumstances?" Stello asked.

"No one knows," replied Nogaro. "No, no one on this side of the Galaxy knows. He lost his ship when he landed on Glania, probably as the result of clumsy handling, and he started on foot toward the planet's Stellar Port, which he reached; the evidence on that score is positive. He had an interview with the commandant of the Stellar Port, but never came out of the commandant's private apartments. Or if he did his destination was unknown."

"And what did the commandant have to say about that interview?" Olryge asked.

"Not a word. He committed suicide. He had allowed a

prisoner to escape and I suppose he went to pieces. Just think: a man with neither ship, food, nor special information who suddenly disappears from an almost deserted planet and who literally vanishes in space."

"Could he have died in some dark corner of Glania?" suggested Albrand.

"No," said Nogaro. "I had a thorough investigation made. There was no trace of him on the planet. Nothing except some fingerprints on a glass that had contained zotl."

· "Where was the glass?"

"In the commandant's office. The investigators found it after the suicide; they made a note of the fingerprints, just as a matter of routine, and they discovered that they belonged to a human named Jerg Algan. But they never realized the full import. I found out about it much later."

"Zotl?" said Fuln. "The commandant was stoned. Perhaps he killed Algan to avoid discovery."

"No, drinking zotl was not illegal at that time. It was outlawed only a century and a half later, when we felt obliged to keep in check the economic power of the Ten Planets."

"A strange story," said Voltan. I don't like stories that are that strange. Nothing good ever comes of them. But does any of this mean anything? Are we worrying about nothing? I don't believe one man can endanger the human Galaxy even if he is immortal. Those days are over. I've seen dangerous men, very dangerous men, but in the past; not nowadays. No, not nowadays."

"What will it take to make you believe it and begin to worry?" shouted Nogaro. "You're too old. We're all too old. Nothing frightens us anymore. We no longer believe in danger."

What is to be, will be, Nogaro thought. *We've done what we could. Men will now have to make out as best they can. If only I knew what was going to happen to them!* Then he thought of Algan. One man, lost, alone in a forest of suns, attaining immortality, and what else? Was the center of life in the center of the Galaxy?

"I have nothing more to add," he said. "I am asking you to set into motion as quickly as possible our plan to achieve immortality for the whole of the human species. I hope it is not too late."

He looked at them, one after the other, and he read on their faces which had been furrowed by time, fear, worry, weariness, habit, boredom.

"You know my answer," said Olryge exultantly.

"I can't," said Stello reluctantly.

"I don't think the time has come," said Albrand.

"No," said Fuln.

"No," said Aldeb, Voltan, and Luran in chorus. They seldom spoke, buried as they were under the weight of memories, crushed by experience.

"Perhaps you're right," said Nogaro. "I hope so. I hope you're not making a mistake."

"We hope so too," they said.

"Is the discussion over? Shall we bring the meeting to a close?" asked Olryge.

"As a matter of fact it would be better to stick to the decision you've made," said Nogaro ironically. "You might do even worse."

Albrand stirred.

"Perhaps we ought to look for this man, this Jerg Algan," he said.

"He's out of our reach," said Nogaro.

"The Machine?"

"The Machine knows nothing. Do you suppose that I am not consumed with curiosity to find out what lies outside the human Galaxy?"

"Don't take it that way, Nogaro," said Voltan. "After all, you're the one who unleashed the danger that you say threatens us."

"I did, and it had to be done," said Nogaro.

"That is beside the point."

"It makes no difference," Olryge exclaimed. "The voting is over."

Voltan turned toward him.

"Don't be in such a hurry, Olryge. Eternity stretches before you. I'd like to ask Nogaro one or two questions."

"I'm listening," said Nogaro.

"What were those stories you mentioned just now?"

"I'm not sure I ought to speak of them here. After all, they were only stories."

"Let's have them."

"Well, they mentioned an empire on the boundary of ours, giant citadels; but we never saw anything. They mentioned the Masters, but they never came; they mentioned a chessboard and the origin of worlds, but they were only stories. I listened carefully for a long time, I believed some of what I heard. Nothing ever came of them, or almost nothing."

"Almost," said Voltan. "You call it nothing; immortality."

"They told of what had existed before man and what would happen after him," said Nogaro. "They were heavy with curses. They said we had taken a wrong turning. They dealt with whom we might meet in the center of the Galaxy."

"Whom?" sneered Olryge.

"The creators of men," answered Nogaro." The Masters of the stars that dominate the Galaxy, from the top of their sun palaces; and that was where I sent Jerg Algan. And when he returns, you may be sure he will have been sent by them."

"Who am I?" he asked.

"Jerg Algan," the Machine replied.

"All right," he said.

He was staring at his reflection which was moving at the end of a luminous space, in dreamlike fashion. He couldn't keep his hands from shaking. He was now near the end of his quest. The stars and the Masters, space and time, had brought him here, right into Betelgeuse, into this palace which was the respository of the whole history of humanity. He was now face to face with the Machine in which rested all human hopes.

It had been an awfully long quest. And suddenly, just as the Machine had predicted, loneliness swooped down on him like a bird of prey. There had been so many years. He had crossed the threshold of time alone, and alone he had survived. The universe, he thought to himself, would never have for him any savor except that of ashes and of the past, and bright as were the stars, they could never pierce the thick fog of time past.

Mankind, he told himself, had, through him, achieved one more quest, an ancient, encompassing, definitive one; in a few hours, in a few days, all humans would have in their mouths that same flavor of ashes as they thought of their useless exploits.

He wondered what would happen to the Machine, to the palace of Betelgeuse, the gigantic statues that adorned the esplanade, the agile spacecraft that hovered over the ports, whose prows had plowed so many different gulfs, whose hulls had reflected the rays of so many different stars.

"Do you want to ask me another question?" asked the Machine.

He did not reply at once. He looked at his reflection and thought he was at last finding his identity after a long search. So that was he, with that thin, somber face; fine, pale lips; bright, dark eyes. And those long, slender fingers would belong to him for an immensely long time. He wondered if the Machine ever thought itself beautiful, if the humans who had built it had also endowed it with an aesthetic sense, if it enjoyed its own brightness, the blinking of its lights, the green lightning flashes that made it quiver. Then he asked:

"Who are your masters, Machine?"

This question had hung in the air for a long time; it had burned his lips, his tongue, and now he could ask it, in peace.

"Men, Algan," it replied unhesitatingly.

Can a Machine be untruthful? he wondered. *Can it lie?* Then the answer came automatically. *Men can lie.*

"No," he said to his reflection.

The reflection did not waver.

"Listen to me, Machine; do you want me to tell you the truth? You're nothing. You're nothing but a piece of scenery. You might at least admit that. I want to see your masters, Machine. At least, tell them so."

"I cannot answer you," said the Machine.

Its voice was still flat, expressionless, even. It was a curious experience, Algan thought, to question a Machine

and to fault it. But, unlike humans, a Machine knew how
to lie. It would never contradict itself and it was impossible to make it take a lie detector test.

It was in some way better and worse than men, more
absolute. It was hypocritical because men had made it so,
but since hypocrisy had been built in, it became a quality;
it was nothing but a possibility; that precluded any moral
judgment.

Was it the same, by definition, for humans? Algan wondered. The Masters had never mentioned it. Yet, somewhere there was a difference. The Machine did not lie to
achieve its own ends; it lied because, on some points, it
had been built not to tell the truth. Men lied systematically in the hopes of attaining personal ends. Men were off
the beam.

He wondered whether a machine, out of gear, would
succeed in lying for its own ends. It was hard to imagine,
but not, perhaps, inconceivable. It could happen, he
thought, if the Machine were caught in a dilemma such as
failing to follow certain directions, and as a result, being
threatened with annihilation.

Perhaps the Machine would destroy itself. Or perhaps it
would admit to the cause of the conflictive situation and
would solve it by adopting an attitude that did not conform with reality. A neurotic attitude.

Humans were forever plunged in a conflictive atmosphere. They existed in order to attain a certain object
which they were prevented from attaining. Some of them,
when the pressure of the conflict became too strong, committed suicide; their instinct for self-preservation—that is,
one of the rules which had been imposed upon them—
vanished. Others sank into a neurotic state. But the equili-
brium of everyone was threatened.

And that explained the history of mankind, those thousands of years of murdering, lying, looting, swindling, war-
ring, and that thirst for conquests and victories, that pas-
sion for power.

Men were Machines out of gear.

"Listen to me, Machine," he said. "You'd better answer
me."

He could not help talking to it as to a human. He

struck his fist against the cold surface of the mirror. He heard a weak vibration which was stilled almost immediately. He could do nothing against the Machine, at least, not that way.

"I cannot answer you," said the Machine.

"I have a message for your masters, Machine. Give it to them. Tell them I want to speak with them. Tell them that I come from the center of the Galaxy. Tell them that I was sent by Nogaro, if they remember his name."

"Men are my masters," the Machine repeated.

Suppose the Machine is telling the truth, he thought. *Suppose it had been built so as not to know who is really giving it directions.* He himself did not know. The Masters, likewise, did not know—or at least did not appear to be interested, which was why he had been sent. But he found it difficult to believe that humans could for whole generations have concealed their power behind so perfect, so efficacious a mask.

What if they refused to see him, to hear him out?

"I'm going to ask you a question, Machine."

"I'm listening."

"How did I get here, to this planet?"

"I don't know. Wait, I'm going to check."

He waited a few seconds.

"You already asked me that question a little while ago," said the Machine. "Why do you want to know?"

"I only want to show you, you don't know everything, Machine."

He wondered if the Machine's mechanical brain could understand his reasoning.

"No mechanism, no being can claim to know everything," said the Machine. "Their function is not to know everything. It is to remember. It is to learn. I must ask you a question. How did you get to this planet?"

"By means of the sixty-four squares," said Algan.

"I see," said the Machine. "I'm missing a lot of data, but a number of possibilities emerge. There could be other Machines like me in space."

"Could be," replied Algan evasively.

"The chessboard is one of the weak points in my reasoning," said the Machine. "I can ascribe certain values to it, but none is predominant."

"Does the problem interest you, Machine?"

"Nothing, in the human sense of the term, interests me. I was made simply to solve a number of problems. That's one of them."

"I know the solution, Machine, and I've come to give it to your masters. Tell them so."

A few seconds went by. This last attempt might fail and he would have to find other means of carrying out his mission. He had hoped that the Machine would serve as a link between him and the hypothetical masters of the human Galaxy. But he was no longer sure.

"I know of no other masters than men," said the Machine. "I cannot solve the problem you have put to me, man. However, my instructions provide for such a contingency. I don't understand them, but I'll follow them. You may be right and maybe some particular men from among all men are my masters. But I can find no evidence of this in the circuits I know. I am going to try to analyze my subconscious ones."

A conflict, thought Algan. *Here at last is a conflict. The Machine is programmed to remain ignorant of certain factors even though it has stored an outline of these factors, and now it seems that the solution to certain problems that it must solve according to basic instructions is impossible because it has neglected this programming. I wonder whether its inventor made provision for this.*

It was exactly the same for men. They knew certain things, but they were incapable of remembering them consciously and expressing them verbally. Result: conflict, suicide, or neurosis.

"You will have to solve the problem by yourself, human," said the Machine. "I cannot help you. My instructions are merely to let you pass."

"Is this the first case of its kind?"

"The first in my memory bank."

Was it possible, Algan wondered, that the Machine had several facets, several faces, that its memory bank was multiple and compartmented? Was it possible that one part of its huge construction was used to answer humans while another was used by the hypothetical masters of the human Galaxy? Was there somewhere a central coordinating place where the final decision was made? Or were the several conscious parts of the Machine separated by ill-defined, gray, unexplored zones?

Could it be that the masters themselves controlled a fraction of the Machine without the knowledge of other centers of the Machine?

"Good luck, human," said the Machine.

Algan's reflection shivered. The surface of the mirror trembled much like an expanse of water over which, suddenly, a breath of air is blown. Then, at the end of the luminous space, a black spot appeared which absorbed all of the light, spread, and gradually devoured Algan's reflection. The blackness now covered almost all of the mirror, conjuring up an unplumbed depth.

It was a door.

He stepped forward and found himself, with no transition, in the night. He put his hands out, then on the sides, but his fingers encountered nothing. He was in the middle of a huge, dark plain.

"Forward," said the Machine.

He concentrated.

Perhaps it was a trap. He was ready to throw himself a million miles away if there was the slightest danger. He knew that he was stepping into a region which few men knew of and which the Machine itself had probably never explored, even though it was located inside the palace. He remembered something Nogaro had said about Betelgeuse. It was, he had said, a gigantic spider spinning its web in time and space, hooking its thread to the stars.

He was going into the spider's parlor. He remembered the trapdoor spiders of the Earth, dragging themselves along into curious holes in the soil that were lined with silk and closed with a hinged lid. A hinged glass. A mirror.

The ground fell away underfoot and pulled him down. He had no way of telling how fast he was moving. All he knew was that he was going where he wanted to. Just as he'd been doing for two hundred years.

He came out suddenly into the light. It seemed to

emanate from the walls of a corridor which stretched out of sight and which must bury itself in the colossal mass of the palace.

The moving belt which had been carrying him came to a stop. He had to walk the rest of the way. The builders of the palace had not wanted it to be fully mechanized. They knew that under certain conditions machines can become dangerous. Algan examined the walls. They were finely polished and made of a hard, cold, white substance. He told himself that he was only crossing to the other side of the real walls of the palace.

Walls hundreds of yards thick.

The palace was a veritable stellar fortress. Its builders had had war in mind. They had thought of men, but also perhaps of other adversaries, more powerful ones, from the stars.

Jerg Algan smiled. He was the equivalent of an invading army and he was sure to win.

The builders of the palace had heard too many stories in their childhood about sidereal fleets invading a planet or about fantastic weapons, bombs capable of destroying half a planet. They had never envisaged attack from one single man.

He walked on faster, the sound of his footsteps on the hard floor echoing sharply. It seemed to him, at times, that the clear sound of his heels came from ahead as if an invisible walker were preceding him. The color of the light gradually began to change. From white to ashen. Even the walls became tinted with gray. He remembered skies in the center of the Galaxy which he had admired, star-studded firmaments which were tinted in the same ashen light, the color of an extinguished fire but which still preserved, for a long time, the intensity, the calm magic of flames.

At last he came to a series of large rooms and he knew he was on the other side of the palace walls. The palace probably had other entrances, less complicated ones, but this one had been built to impress possible future visitors, whoever they might be.

A double row of huge triangular pillars supported a rounded dome. The sound of his footsteps was absorbed by the floor and he felt as though he were burrowing into silence.

He remembered having read once, in some old books when he was still on the Earth, descriptions of buildings similar to these rooms, samples of a now defunct style of architecture. These were nearly as grandiose as the black citadels. In some fields, he thought, men had almost equaled the Masters; but what was the result of tremendous effort for men was only a game for the Masters.

He suddenly came upon a room that had no exits. It was smaller than the ones through which he had just come, and it was empty. He looked around, unable to see any trace of an opening in the walls. Then he noticed a circle engraved on the floor, in the middle of the room.

He had barely stepped into it when, as he had expected, the circle opened up and he fell into darkness.

He was falling slowly without feeling any of the disagreeable effects of a fall. He wondered how deep the well was. He tried to touch the sides by stretching out both arms, but he couldn't.

Was he, he wondered, the first man to go down this passage? Abruptly his feet were on solid ground again. A luminous ray stood out on a black wall facing him. It widened rapidly, and, blinking, he saw a large hall with bare walls, filled with an ashen light.

His heart beat faster. He saw a large, round crystal table in the middle of the room. There were eight men, seemingly dressed in silver, sitting around the table. He walked toward them. Their faces were strange, etched with lines of fatigue.

They watched him silently.

His glance came to rest on one of them and memory stirred. He couldn't believe his eyes. Yet he knew those deep-set dark eyes, those intelligent, somewhat bitter features.

He started to talk.

CHAPTER XI

The Chessboard of the Stars

"Nogaro."

"I was expecting you, Jerg Algan," said Nogaro.

Algan stood in front of the table and stared at the red-headed man whose eyes shone like rubies, and the man smiled.

So, Algan thought, these were the men who ruled the human Galaxy. He wondered what had happened to the merchants of Ulcinor. The Masters had told him to pay no attention to them. Then he looked again at Nogaro. There was only one possible solution. Nogaro was immortal. All these men were immortal. That was why they ruled the Galaxy. The merchants of Ulcinor had imagined another sort of continuity in time based on traveling at the speed of light and on time warps, but these men were completely and genuinely immortal.

They were almost as powerful as the Masters, he thought. Then the idea vanished. Nothing was comparable to the might of the Masters. He remembered certain facts which had surprised him in the past, about Nogaro's activities and about his influence. Now he understood.

"And so you are immortal," said one of the men, leaning forward.

"Just like you, Nogaro," said Algan. "That explains a lot."

"More than you think, Algan," said Nogaro. "It explains the stability of this civilization, the first to withstand the upheavals of history. We are somewhat like the brain cells of an individual, something that remains alive as long as the individual does, as long as this society. And we are well hidden, Algan, just as the brain of a man is hidden inside his skull. But you finally found us."

"After a long detour," he said.

"Why do you feel the need to explain all that to him, Nogaro?" Olryge said. Why not question him instead? I don't suppose he sought us out to hear our story."

"It may be useful for him to know it," said Nogaro.

"And you kept your immortality a secret all this time!" said Algan.

He felt rancor sweep over him. The hatred he had borne for so long inside him became mixed with something colder, less precise.

"And so you succeeded?" Nogaro asked.

"Yes."

"You reached the center of the Galaxy?"

"I reached it." He saw the eight faces focusing on him and a sort of nausea invaded him. His mouth felt dry.

"And you've come back. After two hundred years. Why?"

"I have a message for you."

He disliked the feeling of those looks on his skin. He had forgotten men, and now he saw them, face to face, with no pleasure.

"From whom?" asked Nogaro.

"I have plenty of time; we all do. You'll find out everything."

"Don't try to play games with us," said Albrand. "You successfully carried out a long and dangerous mission, for which we are grateful to you. But don't try any games."

Algan started to laugh.

"I won't," he said hoarsely.

"You're changed, Algan," said Nogaro. "What's happened to you?"

"Yes, I've changed," said Algan. "I am immortal now. But you weren't concerned about that when I left. You weren't concerned then about any alterations that I might undergo. You used me, didn't you?"

"I had no choice. You were willing."

"I don't hold anything against you. I bear you no

grudge. I might have once. But not now. I'm even grateful to you. In a way that you cannot understand."

"I think I understand, Algan," said Nogaro. "I too have lived a long time. And I was, and still am, your friend."

"That no longer matters. Things are going to change, you know."

"Immortality," said Olryge.

Algan shot him a curious look.

"Immortality and lots of other things."

"How did you manage to travel in space?" Olryge inquired. "You had a spaceship, didn't you? A spaceship faster than ours? None of our detectors could pick it up."

"I had no spaceship," said Algan. "And you'll hear how I managed. Don't worry. I came to tell you."

He paused. "To tell you and all other men."

No one spoke. The eight immortals looked at one another.

"The human Galaxy will collapse, if you do," said Stello. "Do you understand?"

Algan nodded.

"Don't think we'll let you do it," said Olryge. "Don't think you've won, even if you are immortal."

"Do you think I'm acting alone?" Algan asked. "Do you think my life is of any importance in what is about to happen? I've only come to give you a friendly warning. That's all."

"Is it an ultimatum?" Voltan asked.

"Did I set any conditions?"

"And so the legends were true," said Nogaro.

"They were not inaccurate," Algan replied. "They just didn't tell the whole story."

"The chessboard?"

"I'll tell you everything; I won't hold anything back," said Algan. "You'll master the chessboard just as I did. That's what I've come to tell you. You and all men."

"Men are not yet ready," said Luran. "As soon as they are, they'll get their immortality."

"What for? Immortality and the chessboard are unimportant. What is important is what I'm going to tell you."

"We're listening."

"It can wait. Have you no questions? Important questions?"

They looked at one another again. Algan could detect a vague fear in their eyes.

"And so, there is a form of life in the center of the Galaxy," said Nogaro.

"Yes."

"And a civilization?"

"Yes."

"More advanced than ours?"

"That depends upon what you mean by civilization and by life. Life and civilization to you signify forms of organization inscribed in space which alter in time along a predetermined course. What exists over there is very different from what you can imagine."

"Are they . . . hostile?"

"Do you mean hostile toward humans? Why should they be? Why, then, send me to you?"

Olryge got up and leaned down toward Algan, supporting himself by his hands on the crystal table.

"You're an enemy," he said. "You were human once. But they have changed you. You're nothing but an empty shell inhabited by a stranger. You've come among us in order to destroy us. But we won't let you."

He slipped his right hand into a fold of his clothing and drew out a slender stiletto which he brandished at Algan. A golden beam flashed out from the point of the weapon and touched Algan's chest.

"No," said Algan. "Those who sent me armed me against this sort of an attack. You can't do anything to me. I, on the other hand, could grab your weapon and turn it against you. I thought you were more intelligent. I thought the years had brought you experience. You're unbalanced. But don't worry. We'll cure you."

"Perhaps you would be good enough to tell us now why you have come back?" said Stello.

"Perhaps I could," said Algan. "Only I wonder if you're ready to hear what I have to say. First, I'd like to tell you what I've done: I've looked at space, with naked eyes; I've stared at stars in all their brilliance, the Galaxy in all its extent and splendor; I've plumbed depths you've never

dreamed of; I've listened to the music of hydrogen; I've
seen light and time flow about me like the waves of an
endless river. All this will be yours, too. When I experienced that, I realized that man had been created not to
live in the dark dens he keeps building on muddy planets
nor to take refuge in steel and glass spaceships, terrified,
cowed by the idea of the universe around him; I realized
he was meant to conquer the universe, but empty-handed
and not just for himself."

"For whom, then?" Olryge asked loudly.

"You'll find out later," said Algan. "And everything I
have seen and experienced will be yours also. But in order
to get it, you'll have to learn a number of things."

He noticed their hands begin to tremble on the crystal
surface of the table. He saw their expressions tense up and
their eyes shine.

"The first part of my message is simple and can be
stated in a few words. But I'm afraid it's going to take
you a long time to accept it."

He stepped back and took a deep breath. He felt the
deepest recesses of his lungs fill with air. He was pervaded
with a tranquil sadness.

"Just one sentence," he went on. "Men are robots."

He heard Nogaro murmur:

"I knew it. I'd always thought something of the sort."

"And those who sent you are our ... builders," said
Stello with some difficulty.

"If you like. Imagine a race that does not think in terms
of years nor centuries nor even millennia, but in terms of
millions of years, for whom the birth, life, and death of a
star represent a duration of time comparable to that of an
individual for humans. Imagine that their hub lies in the
center of the Galaxy. Imagine that they want to stretch
out and fill the surrounding space ... no, not that ...
imagine rather that they want to stretch a web of life, a
web of warmth and intelligence on surrounding emptiness,
that they want to connect those distant points that shine in
the dark, that they want to accomplish what we have called
the conquest of space. They could use spacecraft like
ours, but they could also make use of other means, more
in keeping with their concept of space and time. So they

decide to use machines that will enable them to travel
through space, machines that can make their own complicated calculations that displacement of this sort would re-
quire.

"Imagine, therefore, that they conceive a plan, spread
out over millions of years and calculated to guarantee
control over the whole of the Galaxy; that they realize the
plan slowly but surely, with unruled meticulousness and a
total disregard for the passage of time. This race of beings
moves slowly and ponderously through space in order to
fit together the pieces of the puzzle, somewhat the way
men have sown, a little everywhere in space, fragments of
their own civilization in order to reconstitute an entity
which was known as the human Galaxy.

Just imagine that long, long ago this race decided to
build machines, and in order to do so, scattered, on thousands of worlds, the seeds of life and conditions suitable for
the development of that life, as well as other things that
will turn out to have been necessary. And that they waited,
for a very short time by their reckoning, but an exceedingly
long time by man's reckoning, for these seeds to burgeon
into life. Imagine that this race watched over the development of these sources of life, scattered around the center of
the Galaxy which it occupied; that it saw all kinds of forms
of government succeed one another, as provided for in the
original plan; that it witnessed a great number of failures
caused by infinitesimal divergences in the conditions origi-
nally set forth; but that, broadly speaking, the project was
developing according to plan. Imagine that in these multiple testing grounds, life as we know it was developed, that
multicellular forms won out over protozoa, that animals
derived from plants, that mammals succeeded the great
reptiles, in a gradually more complex sequence of increasingly delicate links leading to the machine destined to insure the control of space to this race of the Creators.
Imagine that man appeared, one day, not just in that one
place in the Galaxy, but in thousands or perhaps even millions of places, and that this story which seems interminable, measured by our standards, lasted barely more than a
second when measured by their race's concept of time.

"Imagine that men then developed at an increasingly

faster rate, still in accordance with the plan which had
provided for shorter and shorter periods of time between
succeeding stages of growth; that men began to conquer,
clumsily at first, with the imperfect means at their disposal, the space around them: first of the world which
bore them, then beyond that world. That they grabbed,
here and there, whole portions of the Galaxy, still ignorant of what they really were and why they existed, not
knowing that beyond the huge abysses of space, other experimental stations had given results much like themselves.
At last, the final stages of the schedule are reached: the
abysses of space that separate the various human empires
shrink from year to year to the point where soon there remain only thin gaps of the unknown that could easily be
bridged by random expeditions or because men are eager
to get to the very regions from which the Creators came,
that is, the center of the Galaxy. Then, one fine day, a
man, a machine, a robot, reaches these regions and the
plan is completed. The huge organization built up in space
by this race is now going to begin to function. Distances
will be abolished; humans will find their true function.

"But will they accept it? That's the problem. Infinitesimal variations in the unfolding of the plan could have
made men forget certain data, neglect others, build up a
disorganized but autonomous civilization.

"Men are machines, but machines that are somewhat
out of kilter. They will need to be repaired, taught what
they have forgotten, given the immortality required to
solve the problems caused by the vastness of space.

"And by a strange irony of fate, or of the plan, these
men were driven by their own problems to build machines
that were quite inferior to those built during millions of
years by the Creators, but the power and intelligence of
man's machines was considerable. Thanks to these machines, they've been able to resolve many problems. Except one.

"Who they were, where they came from, and why they
always turned out, in the end, to be unhappy and malad-
justed; why they continually wished to leap from one
world to another, leave yesterday behind to get to tomorrow.

"But all that was needed was for one of them one day to reach the regions controlled by the Masters; then everything would fall into place. After a brief delay the plan will now finally be fulfilled. Men are going to be able to solve the problems for which they were created; there will be no more neuroses.

"What kind of problem is involved? A problem for which they are particularly well-equipped. A problem which all their civilizations learned to master more or less perfectly. One which appeared to be gratuitous, although actually it touched the very essence of things."

Algan paused.

"The game of chess," he said. "Naturally, men are equipped to solve problems other than those that arise in the game. They must survive as individuals and as a species. They were created to keep themselves in good condition and to proliferate. They are almost perfect machines. The Creators showed admirable ingenuity. They could have invented machines that were more effective in a given field, which functioned faster or with a smaller margin for error, or were longer-wearing: but they would have had to choose. They preferred a sort of synthesis, a machine that was self-sufficient, able to act independently of the exact problem that was put to it, that was capable of moving about, of repairing itself within certain limitations. In some men secondary attributes took over, but they all are able, in varying degrees, to play chess. In order to make the best possible use of men, the Masters need select and train only the most gifted ones, then reject the others, the criteria used being the same as men themselves used when they built their little machines.

"And those dormant attributes of man, those which he had hardly used, can be stimulated by certain drugs. Zotl, for instance.

"The plan, millions of years old, which is in the process of being completed, was based on three things. On certain rules of physics, which make it possible to move through space and which is symbolized by the chess game with its sixty-four squares and its billions of possibilities. On man, who makes it possible to solve the problems arising from movement in space, purely mechanical problems, which

the race that occupies the center of the Galaxy prefers to
leave to others. And finally on zotl, that strange drug
which is essential to the new attributes of man as air or
food are to his vital functions. Through an admirable
economy of means, the Masters have arranged to have
man and zotl be part of the same experiment, or of similar ones, which we call life. Through the use of zotl the
Masters can control men in the conquest of his new attributes. They placed him on worlds other than the ones
on which men were born. This was done so that men
would not discover prematurely the secret of their origin
and of space travel. The Masters wanted man to be ready,
wanted him to have built a civilization in space, just like
yours. That was when zotl was made available to him.

"The game of chess is a symbol. I myself discovered by
using one of those antique chessboards that can be found
in the human Galaxy, that each time a chess problem is
solved, there was a move in space. This is not magic. Man
is properly equipped for travel among the stars, but he has
to know how to use the equipment. The squares in the
chess game represent a certain number of necessary coordinates. For instance, eight squares represent eight dimensions. The solution to a chess problem corresponds to the
solution of a problem of travel in space, and, as soon as
the itinerary has been set, the human body, that most perfect of all spacecraft, plunges amid the worlds, and fol-
lows an almost invisible trajectory at tremendous speed.
There is nothing incomprehensible about that. The Masters made use of the techniques that we discovered much
later and which are used on ships. But they used them almost perfectly.

"They built, millions of years ago, tremendous black citadels which are the magnified equivalents of our stellar
ports. They scattered throughout the Galaxy chessboards
that had been set up. Then they waited. Until now. The
plan is almost completed. The Masters are going to be
able to travel in space, explore the farthest reaches of
space. Their web stretches from star to star. And humans
are going to leap from one point of the universe to another."

"This is inhuman," said Stello in a different tone of voice.

"I wonder," said Jerg Algan. "Do you think it more human to reserve immortality for a small number of the privileged? Do you think it human to strengthen one's power by using men who have been recruited by force? Do you think it human to die wretchedly in the bottom of some poisoned bog on some lost planet under pretext of enlarging the human Galaxy? I think, on the contrary, that we are going to become truly human, that we are at last going to accomplish what we were created for. We are all spacemen, but until now all we've done was to fight space. Tomorrow it will truly belong to us."

"We shall no longer be our own masters," Olryge cried out.

"Have you ever been, except in your dreams? Or were you so because your power crushed millions of men?"

No one spoke. Nogaro's glance wandered over the walls. Thousands of names, he thought. Thousands of names of immortals, a chain now broken. Was it to be regretted?

"The chessboard of the stars," he said. "The black citadels. So, it was all true."

"It was all true," Algan answered. "Somewhere in this planet, a few hundred yards under you, there is a citadel buried under heavy layers on lime and alluvium. You might, by chance, have discovered it. But was it chance that you did not, in fact, do so? Was it by chance that the floor of the great hall in which the Machine is located is an exact reproduction of the chessboard? Was it by chance, also, that you sent me on an expedition to the center of the Galaxy; that one of the shopkeepers gave me an antique chessboard? Sometimes I wonder. The Masters did not tell me."

"A huge network of citadels," Nogaro whispered as in a dream. "And our conquest is pure waste. Those millions of men died in vain. What a mess. And we thought we were so great."

"The time of the mess is over," Algan said gently. "And I don't think we've lost any of our greatness. I believe, on the contrary, that we have at last achieved it. We made a

detour, a much longer one than my trip. As for the network of citadels, that huge spider web spread over space,
there is no absolute need for it. It will be very useful at
first. Then men will learn to travel alone along the wide
paths of space."

"It doesn't matter," said Nogaro. "Whatever happens,
I'll go with you. I want to see the center of the Galaxy. I
want to be present when the human species is transformed."

"Men, robots," said Stello. "I can't get used to the
idea."

"You'll have plenty of time to do so," Algan said with a
smile. "All the time in the world. When you're moving
from star to star."

Olryge brought his fist down on the crystal table.

"You're nothing but a gang of traitors," he shouted,
"and those who sent you, Algan, are nothing but a bunch
of cowards. Oh! I can just see them. They sent you in the
hope that we'd give up without a struggle, that we'd put
ourselves in their hands lulled by enticing tales. I don't believe your story."

"No one is asking you to believe anything," Algan inter-
rupted.

"We won't let ourselves be taken in," roared Olryge.
"What our ancestors predicted has happened. We're going
to have to fight. I, for one, am not complaining. This is
war, Algan, and we'll win. You can go tell that to your
Masters. We're not afraid of them. They won't enslave us
simply because they occupy the center of a Galaxy that
belongs to man."

"There will be no war," Algan said coldly.

He walked up to the table and looked at each one in
turn. Suddenly they felt themselves floating in the air while
a long vibration shattered the walls of the subterranean
room. Their bodies were almost weightless. Olryge gasped.
Luran's hands began to shake. Nogaro remained impassive
and Stello's eyes grew round with surprise.

"The pull of this entire planet's gravity has just been altered," Algan announced. "They can do that. They can
wipe out a star in a second. They would rivet your ships
to the ground. There will be no war. Do you think for one

moment that men will follow you, when immortality and the stars are given to them?"

"But who are they?" Norago asked. "Do they look like men? What are they like? Are they eternal?"

"No," said Algan, "they are not eternal, although their lifetimes are greater than even the entire span of human evolution and history. They know they are mortal. And you know them. Men have always turned to them. . . . They are the stars."

He was silent for a moment, turning over in his mind what he was going to say, scanning their faces, in which he read fear, skepticism, or a strange relief. He could feel the words he was going to speak forming themselves in his head. He had carried them a long time inside him, when he was traveling in space, when he was touching comets and nebulas, when he was exploring man's garden, the universe. His eyes never left their faces as he told them who the Masters were. The stars.

He told them what the stars were, points of light clustered in huge groups which streak the skies like drops of milk dotted on an immense, cold black space; he told them who the Masters were.

They were the stars, or rather something living on the stars, something that was born, lived, and died with the stars, that had appeared a few billion years ago, in the great explosion of atoms, in the shock of billions of particles flung one against another; it was something that had grown slowly in the center of the Galaxy, until it had become a core of consciousness and conscience that yearned to throw light and warmth on the icy emptiness.

He told them about the loneliness of the stars, the extent of which men could neither understand nor conceive: they could only try to imagine it, that determination to link the stars with bonds other than light. He told them that the great plan which had been formulated millions of years ago had only just begun and that, beyond the visible stars, there existed others and that they, men, would be like the intelligence, the conscience, the blood of the stars circulating in the veins of space, unceasingly pushing back chaos, and the cold of darkness. He told them that there were other galaxies and other universes and that men would explore them until the stars were extinguished one by one, and that beyond that frozen death of the universe they would perhaps continue to carry the torch of a glorious stellar existence.

He described for them the beauty of the worlds whirling about in space—which none of them had ever really seen—the splendor of double or triple stars, the magnificence of the skies in the center of the Galaxy, where stars touched and worked together to achieve the great goal that had no beginning and no end.

He explained to them that now for the first time man was capable of dealing with the universe; that he could throw himself into the night and know that so long as he could see the light of one sun, he was safe.

He told them that the stars themselves did not know where they came from, but that they were content to be and to perform their task; that they sometimes thought that their relationship to other, greater beings was the same as men's relationship to them, that perhaps they constituted oases of privilege in the universe; that perhaps they were taking a glorious but silent part in an even greater, and to them, incomprehensible struggle.

He told them about the other men they would meet, about the strange and wondrous worlds they would put into contact with one another, bringing here the flame of life, there knowledge, and the message of the stars; that they would be the eyes and the ears, the voice and the hands of the suns. There was no lack of dignity in serving the stars, he concluded.

He waited and at last read in their faces something that might be understanding.

He told them of the surprising world of crystals, of gases and vapors in space, of the ceaseless movement of atoms in time, and of the tireless combinations of matter.

They were only children, he said. They had to learn again to look at the sky through the eyes of a child. A sky in which multitudinous burning and palpitating spheres would shine. And, abruptly, suddenly, they crossed the threshold of the wide open gates to space and entered, with their eyes still unseeing, the infinity that spread beyond.

DAW∷sf
BOOKS

☐ **THE BOOK OF BRIAN ALDISS** by Brian W. Aldiss. A new and wonderful collection of his latest science fiction and fantasy masterpieces. (#UQ1029—95¢)

☐ **DARKOVER LANDFALL** by Marion Zimmer Bradley. No Earth-born tradition can withstand the Ghost Wind's gale. (#UQ1036—95¢)

☐ **BAPHOMET'S METEOR** by Pierre Barbet. A startling counter-history of atomic Crusaders and an alternate world. (#UQ1035—95¢)

☐ **MIRROR IMAGE** by Michael G. Coney. They could be either your most beloved object or your living nightmare! (#UQ1031—95¢)

☐ **CHANGELING EARTH** by Fred Saberhagen. When Terra's turning point arrived. (#UQ1041—95¢)

☐ **THE OTHER LOG OF PHILEAS FOGG** by Philip José Farmer. The interstellar secret behind those eighty days . . . (#UQ1048—95¢)

DAW BOOKS are represented by the publishers of Signet and Mentor Books, **THE NEW AMERICAN LIBRARY, INC.**

THE NEW AMERICAN LIBRARY, INC.,
P.O. Box 999, Bergenfield, New Jersey 07621

Please send me the DAW BOOKS I have checked above. I am enclosing
$_____(check or money order—no currency or C.O.D.'s).
Please include the list price plus 25¢ a copy to cover mailing costs.

Name_____

Address_____

City_____State_____Zip Code_____
Please allow at least 3 weeks for delivery

☐ **THE DAY BEFORE TOMORROW by Gerard Klein.** To dominate the future—change the past! A prize novel by the
author of Starmasters' Gambit   (#UQ1011—95¢)

☐ **WHERE WERE YOU LAST PLUTERDAY? by Paul Van
Herck.** This unique science fiction satire was a winner
of the Europa Award for Best SF novel.
                                        (#UQ1051—95¢)

☐ **THE BOOK OF FRANK HERBERT by Frank Herbert.** Ten
mind-tingling tales by the author of DUNE.
                                        (#UQ1039—95¢)

☐ **STRANGE DOINGS by R. A. Lafferty.** Sixteen of the most
astonishing stories ever written!   (#UQ1050—95¢)

☐ **MAYENNE by E. C. Tubb.** Dumarest encounters a sentient
planet in his long quest for the lost Earth.
                                        (#UQ1054—95¢)

☐ **THE HALCYON DRIFT by Brian M. Stableford.** A dozen
worlds sought the secret of the Dark Nebula.
                                        (#UQ1032—95¢)

DAW BOOKS are represented by the publishers of Signet
and Mentor Books, **THE NEW AMERICAN LIBRARY, INC.**

THE NEW AMERICAN LIBRARY, INC.,
P.O. Box 999, Bergenfield, New Jersey 07621

Please send me the DAW BOOKS I have checked above. I am enclosing
$_____(check or money order—no currency or C.O.D.'s).
Please include the list price plus 25¢ a copy to cover mailing costs.

Name_____

Address_____

City_____State_____Zip Code_____
Please allow at least 3 weeks for delivery